The
Listening Bench

What Would You
Tell a Stranger
in
Confidence?

Randy Judd

Dedication

I realize it is probably trite to make a book dedication to a spouse. Even if that is the case, I still feel the need.

Connie Meidlinger Judd has been such a support in my efforts to succeed in everything I do, especially as an author. She not only acts as my human thesaurus and spelling expert— when I can't even get close enough for spell check to recognize the word—but she's also extremely honest in her critiques, which I need if I hope to improve.

Thanks, Connie! This is for you♥

Prologue

I'm afraid I may have killed my mother!" she revealed.

"Stop right there! You've read the flyer and you should know that you can't tell me anything that you've done that's criminal," Jonah stated, "and killing someone would definitely fit."

"No, not literally. But I feel my actions and negligence are what led to her death, and it haunts me every day. I'm hoping by telling my story it will somehow, I don't know, give me some peace."

Jonah sat back against the bench. Nestling back in his listening position, he could feel the slats of the bench press into his back. He felt as though the seat—over time—had formed to his shape.

"Please, go ahead."

He had never seen this woman, let alone interacted with her. She sat at the other end of the long bench, the glistening lake of the park directly in front of them. The unnamed, slightly pudgy lady struggled to find comfort on the bench. As the bangs of her short blond hair drooped across her eyes, she immediately swept them back with her fingers to their proper position. Her salon hairstyle was typical of a woman her age She presented herself as someone with a proper upbringing. The professional manner of attire gave the impression that she was well educated, attended church, and recycled. It was obvious though, that she had at least one vice since he could catch a hint of cigarette even on his opposite end of the bench. Overall, his quick assessment was that she was a respectable person, but how could he really know in such a short time?

The blond lady took a deep breath and held it for a second. She was about to tell this stranger a story that needed to escape for almost a decade. It was a tale that would not make her look good in front of him, a complete outsider.

"My mom was a wonderful mother," she began. "Mom had been a stay-at-home mom during my early years. She doted over us kids and we were the center of her world. When we were all grown, she finished her education and became a respected hospital administrator. It was almost as if she knew my dad would die young and leave her to provide for herself. As I grew into adulthood, she was always my biggest cheerleader and was available for me to get advice. Mom was constantly supportive of my career and how I reared my son. The universe blessed me with a wonderful mother.

"After my father died, she never remarried. Her life was full with her career and family. She lived alone in the house she had occupied for forty years. She settled very well at first. I enjoyed going to visit her a few times per week and we talked for hours. She always hated to see me go, but I had my own life to attend to. I treasured my limited time with her."

The woman was dressed in a tailored brown business suit with a skirt. She had broken away from one of the nearby offices. Apparently, she was taking her lunch break to tell her story. Jonah caught her twisting her wrist and glancing to check the time.

"After Mom retired at seventy," she continued, "her health started deteriorating quickly. She had always looked young for her age. I don't know if her career kept her young, but after retirement, she quickly evolved into an old woman. Her arthritis and osteoporosis progressed, forcing her to use a walker. She increasingly needed more help. Although my brothers did the best they could, as the youngest child and only daughter, it seemed that most of the caretaking fell on me."

Jonah rocked slightly and adjusted himself on the bench. He always made sure he looked at people directly so they could see he was genuinely engaged in what they said. He actually did care about these strangers and sincerely wanted to be connected. Even if something tempted him in his peripheral, he always tried to concentrate on the speaker's face unless doing so made them obviously uncomfortable.

The predicted afternoon thunderstorms were still a few hours away, but the thunderheads were already boiling above the western mountains.

The woman continued, "I'm embarrassed to say that my time with her became less enjoyable and more of a burden. I stopped by after work several times per week to help do chores around her house. We hired a housekeeper, but Mom ran her off with accusations of theft and laziness.

"Here's the hard part…" She became glassy-eyed looking inside herself to pull up the courage. She had never told this story to anyone but knew she had to tell this listener, a stranger, in order to deal with whatever her next steps were.

"Go ahead when you're ready."

She was ready. "One day I was cleaning her kitchen and the stress of the day was swelling. I felt as if I had to have a cigarette to relax. I don't know if you've ever smoked, but when the urge calls long enough, you feel forced to answer. Just as I was reaching for the back door to go hide with my cigarette—Mom never approved —, I hear Mom from her bed. 'Can you get the remote for me, dear?'

"'I will Mom. I've got to step out, but I'll be right back in.'

"Being late for a commitment with my girlfriend, Madge, I thought I would use this time to call her and let her know I'd be delayed. Madge can be quite a talker, so I took longer than I should've. After puffing the last hits of my cigarette and flicking it into the yard, I opened the screen door and stepped back in the house."

The lady delicately approached the part of her story that she had never told anyone, even—no, especially—her brothers.

"When I entered the doorway of her bedroom, I couldn't see her. I checked the bathroom, and she wasn't there either. As I walked around the bed, I saw her. She was lying on the floor beside the bed. I called to her while hurrying around to see the complete scene. She had fallen and hit her head on the corner of the bed frame. She was face down by her walker. She was very pale. There was a little blood on her head, and it seemed obvious she was dead. Adding to my pain, resting in her hand was the TV remote."

Her monologue stalled as this daughter began to sniffle and wipe her red eyes. Tears and tissues were not uncommon on his bench.

"I immediately called nine-one-one and held her while the ambulance came. All the time I stroked her hair and apologized repeatedly. She was so frail in my arms. 'Mom, I would've gotten the remote, if only you had waited'.

"If I'd only taken those few seconds to get her remote, she wouldn't have gotten out of bed and struggled with her walker across the carpet. If I'd only taken the time…"

The woman at the other end of the bench wept, not a wailing cry, but resembling the sad cry of someone missing a loved one.

As was his standard procedure, Jonah waited a moment to see if she would say anything else.

"I killed my mother."

He let the silence lay on their encounter for a bit. Sometimes, the silence was as cathartic as the telling.

As was standard procedure, he finally interrupted the silence. "Are you glad you told me?"

"I'm not sure glad is the right word. I just had to tell someone the story, to put it out in the universe, but there was no one I could tell. No one that wouldn't judge me for being so thoughtless."

"Can I ask you a question?" Jonah was always careful in the way he approached people post-confessional. Most people did not come for advice. That wasn't the process. They just want to be heard. Occasionally, though, he had a prompting that something more could be done.

"Let's say for a minute that we know for sure there is an afterlife. How would you say your mom describes you to her new friends? What would she tell your dad about the woman you are?"

After dabbing the corners of her eyes, she let out a sigh and responded, "I suppose she would tell them she was proud of me. She was never shy about reveling in my accomplishments. She would say I took good care of her and made her laugh along the way. She would say I was one of her best friends."

Barely finishing the last word, the woman's crying increased slightly, but she understood she was in a public park. Tears trickled down her cheeks and dropped to her clothes.

"She would say she loved me," she said again between sniffles.

At this point, Jonah led the conversation to its natural close. "So, in other words, she wouldn't say you caused her tragic death, but were an integral part of her happy life?"

"Yes, I suppose so. I hope so."

His organic response was to hug her, but he resisted and generally made it a rule to keep his propriety in these situations. She on the other hand had not made such rules. They both stood and she moved toward him, pulling him close into a gentle hug. For a few seconds, she lay her head on his shoulder and they didn't speak.

"I needed this so much. Thanks for letting me confide in you. I think it will help me move on now."

She said her farewell, slung her purse over her shoulder, and walked away, the low heels of her shoes clicking when she got to the sidewalk.

She felt lucky that there were a few blocks to walk back to work so she could compose herself for the rest of the workday.

Jonah stretched and looked up from his bench to see if anyone else was on the waiting bench. Since there was no one waiting, he stretched and walked around the bench to get his blood flowing. The day was already warm and was going to be hot. He was glad his bench was protected in the shade of the large tree at least until the storms came.

As he slowly wandered around his bench, he reflected on the last few months being a listener. He thought back to how it all began and how it progressed so quickly.

As with so many passions in life, he hadn't chosen this calling, but it had chosen him or at least his decisions led him to discover *the listening bench.*

Randy Judd

Chapter 1

Birth of the Listening Bench

Jonah Freeman had no intentions of becoming a sought-out listener on a bench in a park. Jonah was fifty-five years old and at a junction in his life. The company where he worked had recently been sold. He was a mid-level executive and new company did not need him. He and his wife, Michelle found themselves weighing options about the rest of his life and career. He certainly felt he was too young to retire. He also contemplated in which direction he would go. He loved the work he had done with the company. He had worked his way up from sales associate. Although the sporting goods chain he worked for had been good to him, he always felt under-fulfilled in his career. His daily routines didn't satisfy the deep needs he had in life. Jonah didn't know which way his path would lead at that moment, but he hoped wherever he landed, he would feel actualized.

Jonah and Michelle started going to this park several years before. Liberty Park in Salt Lake City was only about two miles from their house in Millcreek. The park is perfect for their needs; walking, running, bike riding, or just sitting. A one-and-a-half-mile sidewalk and road define the circumference of the park. As with many parks this size, there are several playgrounds and a small lake taking up a few acres near the southern end. Liberty Park is one of the oldest such places in Salt Lake City. These hundred acres were formally a grist mill and farm. Buildings from that era still exist within the park. Aside from the playgrounds, the park contains tennis and basketball courts, pavilions, gazebos, paths, and an abundance of benches.

During the weekdays, the park patrons are mostly adults and families of small children. Various types of people use it for their daily exercise. During the weekends and at night, Liberty Park's users are a more eclectic crowd. The atmosphere of the park takes on a Bohemian feel.

One could expect to encounter drum circles, vender tables of arts and crafts, and a prevalent skunky cannabis aroma.

Jonah and Michelle began their day in the park a couple of times per week. After parking in one of the angled parking places under a tree, they would stretch a bit before starting their workout. They generally began by walking one lap around the park together. Jonah would normally have to bow out the remainder of her workout. Since he had broken his leg many years ago, he didn't have the ability or stamina to go much further. Michelle, on the other hand, had seen all the trees while skiing—thus, had not shattered her leg.

"Are you sure you're ok if I leave you here and run a few laps?" she would considerately ask, even though she knew he would always say yes. That's the way she was.

She ran for another thirty minutes while he sat on the bench and listened to podcasts or read. Sometimes, they would bring their dog, Wilhelm. The dog ran with Michelle for a couple of laps, then sat at Jonah's feet by the bench. Wilhelm was a yellow lab; smart and loyal. The name didn't fit. The name should've been reserved for a Dachshund or German Shephard, but the couple chose the name and it stuck. He was twelve years old and was a child to them from the start.

When Michelle completed her workout, she always returned to the bench and performed her cool-down there. Though in her fifties, she was a fine specimen of a woman. Her lifelong athletic nature had kept her body lean and firm. Jonah still got a thrill watching her. After cooling down, she would take her place close beside him on the bench. They always tried to get the same bench each time. The couple both enjoyed comfortable, predictable things.

Over time, they became acquainted with some of the other regulars in the park. Occasionally, someone stopped by to exchange pleasantries. They knew little about those that shared the park with them, some more than others, but it was nice to have the familiarity.

Their usual bench was a green steel bench that set back fifteen feet from the walking path at the south end of the park. The bench sits mostly in the sun during the morning. By the time the afternoon's rays began to pounce on it, the bench's heat was slowly soothed by the gradually creeping shade of the massive trees nearby. There was nothing between their bench and the lake but fifty feet of lush grass. They enjoyed sitting on the bench for a while when they had the time, both talking with each other and watching the variety of people sharing the park with them.

After that one cold, wet day in October when Jonah's world darkened, he had a hard time bringing himself back to the park and their bench. Muddling through his despair and loneliness, he eventually returned and sat alone for a couple of hours periodically. Aside from their home, this is where he felt her presence most.

On a crisp morning in mid-spring, he sat in his thin windbreaker watching numerous unknown runners, cyclists, and strollers pass by while he listened to a podcast about grief. As he sat, one of the regulars stopped to talk.

Marvin had talked to Jonah and Michelle several times over the last six months before she was taken. He had a Springer Spaniel named Bridget who wanted to sniff Wilhelm's butt. Wilhelm seemed fine with it. They knew some of the basics about Marvin. He had been divorced from his second wife for about twenty-five years and came to the park to walk Bridget and maybe meet someone. He never did and he assumed he never would.

Marvin was in his early sixties, though he looked much older. He tried hiding his balding head by carefully rearranging some remaining hair. Jonah thought that Marvin should just accept his plight and cut his hair short or even shave it. With even an initial glance, one suspected Marvin had a hard life. His face generally drooped from years of sadness. It would take a deep look to find any smile lines on his face. Despite his aged appearance, he did well at keeping himself presentable and well groomed.

"How's it been going, Jonah?" Marvin asked as he bent over to pet Wilhelm—who was busy being greeted by Bridget.

Jonah had grown to hate that question. He tolerated it, though, because most people don't know exactly what to say. He felt he probably wouldn't either if the roles were reversed.

"I'm doing ok, Marvin. I know it will take time," Jonah replied.

Marvin searched for words, "I never know what to say since I've never lost anyone close to me except my dad a few years ago. He had cancer pretty bad, so his passing was kind of a blessing. Mom is still kicking in her eighties."

"It's ok." Jonah said, "thanks for trying."

"Do you mind if I sit a while?" Marvin asked. "I've walked a couple of laps, but don't want to go home yet."

Although it started out cool, it was going to be a gorgeous day at the park the temperature in the high seventies. The sun was out and peaking sporadically through the freshly budding trees. The carpet of grass had relinquished its winter dormancy and emerged bright green while the Wasatch Mountains, only twenty miles away, still hung onto their winter quilt of snow.

Jonah moved Wilhelm's leash and made a space at the other end of the bench. Others had dropped by over the last few months to check on Jonah. Most of his visitors just stood for the quick interaction. It felt odd and uncomfortable to have Marvin sitting next to him where Michelle had sat hundreds of times. He wanted to protest but knew he had no right.

Jonah started the conversation to avoid thinking of Michelle anymore at this time.

"Do you live close by, Marvin?"

"Actually, I live a few miles away," He quickly replied, "I drive over here a couple of times a week because it's such a beautiful place and great for Bridget. It also holds a lot of memories for me. My mom used to bring us kids over here so we could play and get our wiggles out. Those were some fun times in my childhood."

Jonah was normally skilled at maintaining a conversation but really wasn't up to it. He did give him an attentive listening ear.

"Mom didn't have Dad's help most of the time, so it was as though she was a single mom. Dad was a good provider but worked a lot. She did a great job at being our mom. I know a lot of people complain about their childhood, but not me. Mom did everything she could to make sure we knew we were loved. She made sure all her kids were polite, did well in school, and worked toward a good education and career. She is a good woman, a saint!"

"You're lucky to still have her, Marvin," Jonah said.

"Oh, no doubt. I don't know what I'll do when she's gone. I do a lot to take care of her."

"When she passes, you'll be comforted in knowing that you loved her, and she loved you," Jonah said as if he had an abundance of wisdom, which he didn't. He did have a similar experience with his dad, though.

"I know you've been single for a while. Do you mind if I asked if you have anyone that you're seeing now?" Jonah pried.

"No, not really. I've dated off and on since my last divorce but never could get committed to it. I was afraid some things in my past would prevent me from building any type of meaningful relationship."

Awkwardness settled in swiftly. Jonah didn't know if Marvin expected him to ask, or would he prefer him not? He paused which made the awkwardness even worse.

For a few minutes, no words were uttered. They both just sat in silence and watched the dogs. The canine friends had fallen asleep sprawled out on the new grass. Men can generally get away with silence easier than women. They can comfortably sit for several minutes with an occasional grunt and still be just fine. Most women seem to feel a pause in conversation is a social travesty and needs to be filled before anyone notices.

Finally, Marvin broke the silence, "Jonah, do you mind if I share some things with you, things I've not talked about to anyone else in years? I don't know why exactly, but you seem to be the kind of person who is a good listener and hopefully won't judge me for things I'm wanting to tell you."

Jonah was perplexed why Marvin would make this assessment. They hadn't interacted enough for the two to know each other's conversation skills. Sure, they had talked several times, but their conversations were never very substantive. He must've made that assessment because of something in the way Jonah reacted while listening. Actually, Jonah had been told over the years that he was a good listener. One of his metaphysical friends had tried to read his aura once and said he had a deep soul. Whatever that meant.

"Well, I suppose you could tell me. If you want to share, I'll be glad to listen."

"Great, thanks, Jonah.

"Back in the eighties, I was an up-and-coming CPA. I was working for a national firm in their regional office here in the city. I felt successful. I had graduated from the university as had my siblings.

"My family members were all proud of me. They each had done well in life and Momma and Dad were proud of each of their kids.

"I got involved with a lady and we got married quickly, but it only lasted a year. Our divorce was drawn-out, painful, and in the end, she left me with a mountain of debt, legal fees, and alimony to pay.

"Since financially it was more than I could handle, I got desperate to get more money as quickly as I could. I took a job on the Alaskan Pipeline with the intention of making a lot of money in as short of time as possible, pay off my debts, and return to being an accountant here in Salt Lake."

Marvin took a break in his story and took a drink from his water flask. He closed it, then continued recounting his adventure.

"The money was great in Alaska, and I was able to work all the overtime I could handle. My plan was working great until one night when I slipped on some ice in front of my hotel room and broke my arm. It was bad enough that I couldn't work. Then, after several weeks, it became obvious that I was addicted to the pain medicine. I was using all my Alaska earnings to feed my habit. I even started dealing a little in pain meds to supplement my savings. Things continued to go downhill. I couldn't afford my hotel room and actually became homeless for a while in Alaska.

"I eventually made my way back to Utah and filed bankruptcy. I was able to get another job as an accountant, but my addictions continued to haunt me. I couldn't keep a job for very long. By the time I finally got cleaned up, I had burned all my bridges and could only find part-time bookkeeping work.

"Of course, my family never knew the whole story, but they knew I had returned changed. As a soldier coming home from war, they knew I hadn't returned the same man I had left. They assumed it was because of the divorce and the devastation it had. I never talked specifically about my situation, and out of respect, they never asked.

"It's something I've carried with me for years. I've wanted to tell someone…to confess to someone. I'm not a religious man, so I didn't have a priest or anyone to go to.

"Over time, I got clean and regained my life to some extent, but my demons have kept me from giving my all in any relationship. My second marriage failed after five years. I've given up on getting married again. I'm a confirmed bachelor just not totally by choice.

"I live with Mom, and I find most of my worth in taking care of her, which isn't all bad. I do worry about when she is gone and what I can do to feel worthy in life.

"Now that I've told you my sad life story, I hope you don't judge me too harshly, but I just had to tell someone."

When Marvin finished this abbreviated version of his life, Jonah wasn't sure what the man wanted from him. He couldn't just sit there and stare at Marvin, but he also didn't know if he sought advice or what.

Finally, Jonah decided to give him the least committed response he could, "Marvin, now that you've told me, how do you feel?"

Marvin thought for a while and responded, "you know, I feel really relieved. I feel as though I've just let out a huge sigh. I feel amazingly free. Thank you, Jonah! Thanks for letting me reveal my baggage. I've been carrying this around for so many years."

"I didn't do anything but listen," Jonah replied.

"Yes, but that's actually all I needed just someone to listen. We'll never bring this up again, right?"

"Of course not," he answered.

"Just as I thought, you are a great listener. Thank you."

As they said their goodbyes, Jonah contemplated how good he felt. He hadn't done anything but sit on the bench and listen, but that was all Marvin needed. By just sitting there paying attention to the man, he had fulfilled a need and it was really easy to make a difference in the other man's life.

Jonah probably wouldn't have thought much more about his time with Marvin until a similar interaction happened the next time he was in the park.

Chapter 2

Pam

A few days later, as Jonah was walking Wilhelm around the perimeter, he was passed by one of the other regulars that he and Michelle had met during the time they spent in the park. He struggled to remember the girl's name but came up with it just as she ran up beside him.

"Good morning, Jonah and Wilhelm!" she greeted while only slowing her jogging stride a little.

"Good morning, Pam!" He said as if he hadn't had to struggle to find her name only ten seconds earlier. "How's the jogging today?"

"Well," she answered as she looked back, "I'll let you know in thirty minutes. I'm on my first lap."

Pam was then on her way as Wilhelm stopped to use the bathroom which Jonah dutifully cleaned up. It was, after all, his park.

Jonah admired Pam. She was in her early thirties. She was slightly chubby which made him respect her regular jogging even more. He was sure it wasn't easy to get motivated so often and apparently see very little result, except maybe mentally. Jonah and Michelle had talked to Pam occasionally over the last year, but only small talk. They knew that she was a nurse in a nearby clinic, but little else.

After their lap, Wilhelm and Jonah took their place on the bench. Wilhelm made his obligatory circle before practically falling to the ground and letting out a sigh near his master's feet. Jonah pulled out his phone, put his earbuds in and continued listening to his podcast. He got bored with it quickly and changed to classic rock.

He dozed off to an Eagles ballad but woke up after feeling Wilhelm's leash tighten. When he opened his eyes, he could see Pam petting Wilhelm. The dog's tail was going so fast and powerful it probably created a breeze. Jonah removed his earbuds.

"Sorry to disturb you, Jonah," Pam apologized. "Wilhelm was looking up at me with those big longing eyes as I passed, and I just couldn't deny him a rub."

"No problem," He replied, "fact is, I think he gets tired of me being the only one to give him any attention."

"Do you think he misses Michelle?" She cautiously asked.

"I know he does. Sometimes he'll stand by the front door as if he still expects her to come home."

"Ahh, poor guy," she said while scratching the dog's head.

Pam changed the subject. "Hey, Jonah, I was talking to Marvin yesterday. He was telling me about having a conversation with you a couple of days ago. He, of course, didn't tell me what it was about, but he said it really helped him get past what his issues were.

"He said you were a great listener, and he didn't feel judged in the least."

"It was easy," Jonah stated, "I pretty much just sat and let him talk."

"Sometimes that's the best thing to do," she replied.

She continued, "How would you feel about doing it again, but with me?"

He hesitated a little before answering. "Well, I guess as long as you aren't going to tell me you robbed a bank or something similar," he quipped.

"But if you want to give it a try, have a seat." He pulled his belongings towards him, giving room for Pam to join him.

Pam certainly wasn't stunning in looks. She was short and rounded. Not obese, but certainly living in that neighborhood. She wore no makeup and her dishwater blonde hair fell to her shoulders. If you looked directly at her face, she had a roundish little girl face that was actually quite pleasant on which to gaze. Her resting face retained a lingering smile.

She sat down, opened her water bottle, and took a couple of large drinks. "How does this work? Do I just begin my story?"

"I'm guessing there are no rules. Just tell me what you want me to know," Jonah replied, "the way I see it, you aren't really telling me, you are just putting it out into the universe, and I happen to be the one it's directed at."

She thought, and then said, "That seems about right. Ok, here I go!"

"I'm afraid I made a huge mistake a couple of years ago and let the love of my life slip through my hands," she began.

"Go on," he encouraged.

"I've never had a lot of men interested in me. It's pretty much my lot in life. I've learned to be happy with my job, friends, nieces, and nephews, but there is no doubt that I think about romance occasionally and feel it has passed me by. Understand, I don't NEED a man, but if the right one came along, I wouldn't boot him out, if you know what I mean."

Jonah nodded, focusing on her story.

"As I was saying, two or three years ago, I met a guy at a house party. Similar to me, he wasn't in a relationship and hadn't been for a while. We sat and talked on an outside patio. The conversation was so easy. I didn't feel as if we were posturing or trying to impress. It was so natural for us to be ourselves. We were so engrossed in each other that the party's host actually had to ask us to leave at the end of the night. Oliver was from Britain and had a wonderfully engaging Harry Potter-ish accent.

"We exchanged phone numbers and started talking daily. Eventually, the calls progressed to dating and then a full-blown relationship."

He nodded again to let her know he was invested in her story.

"We dated for a few months. I may put on an 'I don't care' attitude, but I'm actually very romantic at heart. I asked him one night where he thought our relationship was headed. He stammered and stuttered at the question. He then explained that he had previously been in a serious relationship that had ended horribly, and he needed time to process a new relationship. He just needed to carefully see where it went.

"I wasn't ok with his answer. I got a little frustrated and told him that I needed to know that our relationship was worth investing the effort. I knew this was kind of an immature way of putting it. I regretted it. The following day, I was going to Ohio for my sister's wedding. I was going to be gone for a week. In a huff, I told him to think about it and we'd talk more when I got back. I left without even a goodnight kiss."

Jonah hated to interrupt her, but Wilhelm started barking at a squirrel, so he excused himself and asked her to hold her thoughts as he calmed his canine. He hurried back so she wouldn't lose her momentum. In fact, he was interested in her story and wanted to hear more.

"I'm sorry for that interruption. Please continue."

"The whole time I was in Ohio, I yearned to talk to him, but my stubbornness wanted to make a point, so I didn't. On the flight back to Utah, I became resolute in what my actions would be. I knew that I couldn't rush him. I knew that any commitment that was forced was not a commitment at all, but only appeasement. Oliver was the best connection that I had ever had, and I couldn't lose him because of my impatience.

"The first thing I did when the plane landed was to call him. The call went to voicemail, so I left him a message and waited anxiously for the return call. When I hadn't heard from him by that night, I started to worry; worry about him and worry about our relationship. I texted and called again. The call still went immediately to voicemail signaling the phone was probably turned off. I couldn't help but question, had I really screwed up?

"By the third day of not being able to reach him, I decided to go to his apartment. I had shed many tears thinking about what I may have done. If he didn't want anything to do with me, I at least needed to hear it from him. My heart ached for it not to be true.

"His roommate, Jim, answered the door. He told me that Oliver had suddenly left without a lot of explanation. Only that he felt an urgency to get back to England. The roommate said he would give Oliver a message if he called, but he didn't know how to get hold of him. The phone he was using belonged to his employer, so he had to get a new one when he got there, and Jim didn't know his number."

At this point, Pam stopped to compose herself. Jonah could tell that she was devastated in telling the story. She had gone from just tears trickling down her cheek to a heartfelt cry. She reached into her running bag and pulled out a small packet of tissues. While dabbing her tear, she peeked out of the corner of her eye to make sure others in the park weren't aware. After a few minutes, she was controlled enough to continue.

"Jonah, I never heard from Oliver again. It is the saddest story of my life and I've always wanted someone to tell. I haven't had another relationship since then. I may have only had one chance at love in my life. I've always wondered whatever happened to Oliver and why he felt he needed to leave so quickly."

That same awkward silence set in, at least awkward for Jonah. He didn't know whether he should give advice, hug her, just stare at her, or what. Luckily, she broke the silence and ended his indecision.

"Jonah, you've done exactly what I needed. You've just listened. I was embarrassed to tell my close friends or family the whole story. I just needed to get it off my chest and tell someone."

He still felt the need to at least say something, "Do you still hope to find him?"

"No," she replied, "I mean, I think about him often, but I'm also a realist. I know he has moved on and I'm probably just a distant memory to him. For the most part, I've moved on too. I have to. How pathetic would I be if I didn't move on and let it cripple me emotionally for the rest of my life?

"I can't help but think, though, what might have been."

She collected her emotions and her belongings, dried her eyes, and thanked him for listening to her. Before she walked away, she turned back to him.

"Jonah, you know you're a really good listener. You didn't interrupt. I could tell by your expression that you were engaged in what I was saying. Michelle was really lucky to have you as a husband."

That of course made him happy. "I hope she felt that way. I know I was the lucky one to have her."

Pam continued, "the world needs a place where people can go and just be heard. Maybe that's what you can do, sit here all day and listen to people tell you their secrets." In the middle of her flushed face, a sweet smile was aimed at Jonah.

As she walked away, he noticed a happier bounce in her stride. Jonah thought more about what she said He decided to ponder on the idea for a bit.

There was a place in England he had heard of where people could go talk to complete strangers about themselves. As he remembered, they called it the Listening Bench. He looked it up online that evening and found that it had been quite therapeutic for lonely people.

Jonah had a hard time sleeping that night. He just couldn't turn off his brain. He had been looking for something to do where he could make a difference in the world. At 3 a.m., Jonah bought an eBook on Amazon about developing listening skills. He completed it by 7 a.m. There were some very insightful tips in the book but nothing that would be difficult to implement with practice.

As the morning light beams raced over the mountains and tiptoed across his yard, he decided to move forward with Pam's idea.

The bench where he had talked to Marvin and Pam was probably not private enough for these types of conversations, so he chose a bench that faced the lake and gave some privacy. It was several feet behind his and Michelle's bench.

He decided to make flyers to put up around the park. Perfecting the flyers took almost as long as reading the book even though the flyer was only one page.

He knew it wasn't great, but English was never a strong subject in school, so he felt adequate at his attempt.

Need Someone to talk to? Is something weighing on your mind that no one knows about? Do you just need to get something off your chest?

I'll Listen!

I sit on the bench facing the lake at the south end of the park.

Monday, Wednesday, and Friday 9-1

All conversations are held confidential

Only Rule-No confessions of crimes.

He knew it wasn't great—he was sure capitalization and grammar might be wrong—but he just needed something to tell his message.

In the park, there are three bathroom areas, one on either end of the park and one in the center. On Saturday, he placed a few flyers on the outside walls of each bathroom. On Monday, he sat with Wilhelm and waited to see what would happen.

It wasn't surprising to him that nothing happened immediately. People needed time to process what he was offering.

Jonah sat on the bench wearing a light jacket. He decided to walk around a little to relieve some pain in his formerly injured leg.

Jonah Freeman was a good-looking black man standing about five feet ten inches tall. Aside from a little bit of belly paunch, he still resembled the athletic, outdoor man he had always been. He had short curls of salt and pepper color.

His attire had always been outdoorsy; a little Eddie Bauer, a little REI. Today was no different.

He walked to the edge of the small lake in the park and looked across. He was hardly aware of the squawking of the mama duck protecting her babies only twenty feet from him.

Randy Judd

As he stood there on the edge of the little lake, he became nostalgic, He thought of his past, growing up in Colorado, and of his family. It made him smile gently. So many random events had brought him to this place in life.

Chapter 3

Growing Up

Both of Jonah's parents were teaching at the University of Colorado in Boulder when he was born. Phillis York was a professor in the Economics program. She had gotten her Ph.D. from The University of Texas, an eight-hour drive from where she had grown up in Arkansas. She was a very sweet woman, but also stern. Around campus, her classes were dreaded because Dr. Freeman lectured as if she were a judge, and the classroom was her court. Her children did not fear her. They always felt her love, albeit in a somewhat detached way.

Phillis was tall and had a very dark African completion. Her long neck elongated her whole appearance. She was thin and always wore stylish business attire on campus. Knowing that there were only a few black professionals on campus, Dr. Freeman felt an obligation to represent her people well.

Jonah's father, Abel Freeman, was an Assistant Professor in Electrical Engineering. Abel's father had been killed in World War II and Abel's patriotism inspired him to enlist after high school to fight in Korea. The time in the service gave him the opportunity to use the GI Bill to fund his college degree. This was a good thing since Abel's mom had stayed single and barely supported the family. The dream of going to college would've been unrealized had it not been for veterans' assistance. He eventually earned his master's degree at Colorado State University just up the road in Ft. Collins.

On campus, Abel always dressed in his buttoned-up shirt adorned at the top with a tidy bow tie. He had a fun personality with a quick wit. His students enjoyed his antics but knew he would not tolerate mediocrity.

Jonah's mom and dad were great parents for the most part, and he had an average middle-class childhood. Although not poor, his parents were extremely frugal. They had been born at the end of the Great Depression and were part of a generation that was taught to *Fix it up, Wear it out, Make it do, or Do without.* Their cars were never replaced because of model changes, only because they could no longer be repaired. Clothes were meant to be handed down at least one time. Food rarely came from a restaurant, but instead, their table was set with freshly prepared food, mostly from the garden. With both parents working, the children were required to help around the house and as such all of them developed a good, however reluctant, work ethic.

Of course, with both parents being professionals, they made a secure income for the family, but they never displayed it. The money they saved from their frugal discipline was used to ensure their family had great experiences: travel, camps, youth activities, and private lessons. Phillis was known to say, "The only way to really live life is through experiences. Without personal experiences, you are just a spectator of life."

The Freeman parents had three sons, Isaac, Joseph, and Jonah. Ironically, the sons were all named after biblical characters even though the parents weren't necessarily religious. The sons were close in age, and Jonah was the youngest. Although he was the youngest, he was also the most active and brave. Jonah never walked away from a dare and his brothers never walked away from daring him. He was the least likely to give up on a challenge and the most likely to be injured from said challenge.

Living where they did, at the foothills of the Rocky Mountains, the boys were introduced early to the great outdoors. The parents loved to camp, hike, and fish. The boys' childhood was filled with long weekend trips to the mountains and in the summer, an annual week stay in some primitive area above 10,000 feet. Their dad used to say that they were so far in the wilderness that *Bigfoot had grainy pictures of them!*

The town of Estes Park became their sacred jumping-off point to their adventures in Rocky Mountain National Park.

Isaac and Joseph both had summer jobs at the Stanley Hotel in Estes Park. This hotel would later be used as the setting for the movie, *The Shining*, but to the Freeman family, the hotel was just a familiar place where they enjoyed eating Sunday brunch a few times per year.

Aside from the importance of life experiences, the parents also stressed the value of education. The boys were expected to follow their parents' example, graduate college and possibly attain higher degrees. This expectation wasn't a challenge for the two older brothers who graduated near the top of their high school classes and sailed through college in four years.

Jonah, on the other hand, did not develop a love for formal learning. It wasn't because he didn't want to emulate his parents and siblings, he just struggled with things his brothers found easy. It wasn't uncommon for his parents to be called into the school to meet with teachers or the principal. His mom and dad couldn't seem to understand how one of their children could struggle with academics so much. Attention Deficit Disorder wasn't diagnosed at the time. Later in life, Jonah thought that he would've been diagnosed if it were. It would've explained so much.

The youngest boy's happiest place was in the outdoors. As he got older, he had more interest in skiing, kayaking, and rock climbing and less interest in math, science, and social studies.

All the brothers shared a friend relationship growing up. With the minimal African American boys in Boulder, they stuck together and stood up for each other when needed. The boys could be found in the mountains almost every weekend together. The Freeman parents were delighted in the friendship their sons had developed.

What Jonah lacked intellectually, he made up for in common sense. Inversely, his brothers were blessed with intelligence but were sometimes lacking in sensibility. More than once the little brother found himself perplexed by their actions.

One such incident happened soon after Isaac graduated from high school. The boys convinced their parents to let Isaac drive to the California coast with both of his brothers. He was eighteen, Joseph was sixteen, and Jonah was fourteen.

The family had only been to the coast one time before, so they were naturally excited for the delight of the sand, ocean and especially girls.

After a night in Barstow, California, the boys continued driving their mom's Toyota Celica toward the coast, arriving in Malibu by early afternoon. After marveling at the beauty of the coast and playing in the water for a while, Jonah asked a simple question, "where are we staying tonight?"

There was unexpected silence. Isaac looked at Joseph and Joseph held the gaze of his bigger brother. "I guess I thought we would find somewhere once we got here," Isaac lied to cover his blunder.

After almost two hours of calling from a payphone outside a roadside motel that had a neon 'No Vacancy' sign buzzing in the window, the manager of the motel came outside. He had been the one who had told them to use the pay phone two hours before.

"Hey guys," he interrupted. "If you go up the coast about ten miles, you'll see a sign for Hideaway Beach. No one really goes down there after dark, and you should be able to just sleep on the beach and no one will bother you."

The boys were very accustomed to camping, so they felt as though they could sleep almost anywhere. They found the beach, unpacked sleeping bags, and spread out on the sand by the headlights. The salt air wafted across them; the scent was foreign but pleasing. After turning off the lights they snuggled up to the soothing sound of the crashing waves, a lulling sound to which they were not accustomed. The full moon was rising in the east and shining on the ocean creating a night glow over the dark abyss.

The day had ended up being long for the boys. Aside from the long drive, they were fatigued from the stress of not having a place to sleep. About ten minutes after turning off the lights, just as the two younger boys were falling asleep, Isaac jumped up screaming! Joseph and Jonah were both startled, unsure of what was happening. Isaac ran to the car and switched on the headlights. The beams of light illuminated the flat beach immediately ahead. The beam exposed not just sand, but hundreds of tiny crabs, randomly careening across the beach. The spider-like creatures were on the blankets, shoes, pillows…everything!!

In the Rockies, the boys had learned to deal with all manner of animals; skunks, snakes, raccoons, and bears, but knew nothing about ocean life. The ten-legged spiny beings were from an unknown world to the boys. After popping their feet off the sand as if they were stepping in hot tar, they made their way back to the car. With little other choice, they spent the rest of the night sleeping in and on the little Toyota. Jonah was in the front passenger seat, Joseph scrunched up in the back seat, and Isaac (being too tall to sleep comfortably in the driver's seat) slept on top of the car.

The next morning, those same soothing sounds of the waves seemed especially loud. Joseph was the first to recognize their dilemma. He screamed a high-pitched squeal that would have been expected from a prepubescent girl and not a boy in high school. As Isaac and Jonah raised their heads, they quickly shared his terror. During the night, the tidewaters had risen and now encircled their car in a salty prison. Celica Island seemed so far from the beach that their first thought was that they would need to be rescued.

After more thoroughly surveying the situation, they realized the water was no more than two feet deep. With all the energy they could muster, the two older brothers pushed while Jonah guided the car out onto the dry beach. The devil crabs from the night before were nowhere to be seen, but Jonah felt the crabs were laughing at them from the crevices in the rocks.

Once the brothers regained their composure, Jonah chastised his older brothers, "What kind of idiots take us halfway across the country without a place to stay and then park us on a crab-infested beach at low tide?!!"

From that day on, Jonah often referred to Isaac as *My Brother Piñata*, because sometimes you just wanted to hit him with a stick!

It didn't take long for the boys to be able to laugh at the story and forever after, they seldom got together without talking about being stranded on Crab Beach.

Chapter 4

His Road Less Traveled

In the summer of Jonah's senior year of High School, he got a job at *Mountain Impact Sporting Goods* in Boulder. The company was based in Salt Lake City where the family had gone skiing many times. Even though this was his first job, he couldn't imagine a better fit. Not only did he enjoy the pace and lack of structure, but he had more knowledge of most of the equipment than many seasoned employees. The high schooler quickly became the *go-to* for many of the customers and even some employees.

When school started up again, he convinced his parents to let him continue to work part-time. They—mostly his mom—were against it, but finally succumbed to his pleadings.

As his senior year continued, it became pretty obvious by his grades and SAT scores that he—unlike his brothers —wouldn't be accepted to a major college. Isaac had gone to Stanford and Joseph had started attending Purdue.

Jonah's professor parents were disappointed when his plan had to include going to a community college first and then transferring to a university. Even there, he discovered school wasn't his passion and his success would be charted on a different path than his siblings. Luckily, he continued working at Mountain Impact and was able to start working full-time. Jonah moved out of his childhood home and shared an apartment with a couple of buddies.

His academically focused parents' disappointment was always just beneath the surface, but he never felt they loved him any less. They were reluctantly supportive of most things their son did.

Jonah did receive a simple confirmation of his dad's love many years later before Abel died. His death wasn't a surprise. He had dementia and his good days became further and further apart. The last time his son came to see the dad, Phillis met Jonah at the door of his father's room.

She had a hopeful smile when she said, "you've caught him on a good day. I'll leave you two alone."

A good day for the Abel simply meant there were some lucid moments amongst his moments of not recognizing people or being lost somewhere in his childhood.

"Hey Dad," he said softly so as to not startle him, "it's Jonah".

He looked at Jonah and said, "I know who you are, you're my baby boy."

His assurance made the son swell with love toward him.

The eighty-year-old's countenance quickly turned and he spent the next twenty minutes trying to remember where he had left his Buick— the first car he had after high school.

In his fifties at this point, Jonah patiently walked him through the episode.

Suddenly, as if he had just stepped back into the room mentally, the father looked at his son and uttered, "I am very proud of the man you've come to be, Son. I love you."

The only words he could choke through were simply, "I love you too, Dad."

Abel then drifted off into another world mentally. A few days later, he died. Jonah was so glad that the last interaction had been so perfect.

When Jonah got his first car, it was no surprise that he got a 1977 Jeep CJ-5 with a removable top. Under the mud, dents, and scratches, its color had once been burgundy. He named his Jeep, 'Chelsea Jane' (CJ). The teenage boy teased people by saying that he enjoyed taking Chelsea Jane's top off. Jonah drove Chelsea Jane for many years until it seemed she was being held together with wire and duct tape.

Jonah dated off and on during his teenage years. Sarah was his high school sweetheart. To say she was his sweetheart may have been an overstatement. They weren't in love. The arrangement was generally just for careless teenage fun and sex.

The most important lady in Jonah's life was always Mother Nature and she was a jealous lover, so he didn't wander far from her trust too often.

At the sporting goods store, he advanced quickly. By the time he was twenty, Jonah was Department Manager over hiking and camping.

In the spring after his promotion, he was invited to attend a meeting at the company headquarters in Salt Lake City. The meeting itself was held at Alta Ski Resort. Looking around at the beautiful and rugged Wasatch Mountains, Jonah knew he could love this setting as much as his familiar stomping grounds back in Boulder. At the meetings, he was able to meet many of the officers of the company. His boss had told him that it's always good to get his face in front of the right people so they would remember him in the future. His manager turned out to be right.

On the last night of the meetings, all the attendees of the conference went to Alpine Steakhouse at the base of Big Cottonwood Canyon. The restaurant was nicer than the places he was accustomed to eating. The building itself had the appearance of a magnificent log cabin. The theme was continued inside where a guest could easily feel they were in a posh hunting lodge. Heads of local wildlife hung high on the walls and watched as their fellow creatures were devoured on the tables below.

Jonah's parents had periodically taken the boys to formal restaurants—for example, the Cascades Restaurant in the Stanley Hotel—as they passed through their teenage years to make sure they were prepared with the social skills and etiquette for occasions such as this.

Dressed a little nicer than normal, Jonah wore a new pair of khaki pants and a white oxford shirt. The organizers purposely sat the young managers in amongst the executives. Jonah was fortunate—or unfortunate—enough to sit across from the CEO and next to one of the VPs. He made sure he followed the lead of the others as they all progressed steadily through the meal. Throughout the meal, he stayed aware of every question he answered and every bit of conversation in which he engaged. Still being an amateur at social protocol, he, unfortunately, ordered a rack of ribs which were hard to handle with grace. Nevertheless, he was careful not to eat them as the carnivore he was but instead take small, deliberate bites. Being focused on every move, he made sure he wiped his hands often on the linen napkin which was placed discreetly on his lap.

At the end of the meal, after dessert and coffee, Jonah started to rise with the rest of the group to head toward the exit. As the VP next to him put his linen napkin on his plate, Jonah also reached for his napkin to mimic the executive's move.

Jonah suddenly felt the world around him stop for a few seconds. To the boy's horror, there was no napkin on his lap. It had fallen sometime during the meal as he was concentrating on the conversation. He was afraid of what he would see when he looked down and soon felt justified in his fear. On the front of his khaki pants were hand streaks of barbecue sauce as if a bear had mauled him with its bloody claws!

Not usually one to be embarrassed easily, Jonah was humiliated for his blunder to be discovered. The restaurant was dark, so he was able to shuffle to the door holding his jacket over his lap.

Jonah worried about how odd he must've looked to be shaking everyone's hands with his right hand while his left hand held his coat at his crotch.

Luckily, he got away with the gaffe until he and his boss returned to their hotel. The boss stopped, looked at the young man's pants, then back to Jonah's face, and just shook his head with his hand on his forehead and a grin on his face.

The manager held that story over Jonah for several years but luckily didn't tell it often.

Not having seen his bar-b-que stripes on his pants at the restaurant, the Mountain Impact executives had been impressed with Jonah. In the winter of his twenty-second birthday, he was offered a promotion to Assistant Manager at a new Mountain Impact Sporting Goods being opened in Midvale, Utah. Loving his current job and knowing he would probably never return to school; he was excited about the adventure and felt the self-confidence to believe he could succeed.

Jonah's parents, of course, wished he would reconsider school. They also knew him well and loved him enough to support his passion. They had to realize that their own love for the outdoors was part of the reason he was taking a different path in life.

January 15, he loaded up a small U-Haul truck and pulled Chelsea Jane to his new life journey along the Wasatch Mountains in Utah, not knowing what the rest of his life might be.

The Salt Lake City area was not much different than where he had grown up. he could get to six different world-class ski resorts within thirty minutes. In the summer, the hiking, camping, mountain biking, and such were right at his front door.

The young man was ready for his new adventure.

Chapter 5

First Week on the Bench

Unfortunately, Jonah didn't have anyone show up to the bench on Monday after he posted the flyers. He randomly sat, stood, and walked around the bench. He nodded to strangers who may have potential confidences to share. In his boredom, he even came up with a name for the people who would sit and tell their secrets. He decided to call them *Fides*, short for confide. Both Marvin and Pam stopped by to wish him good luck. He joked with Marvin that he was Fide number one and always would be. Pam, of course, was Fide number two. They said they would tell their friends and make sure his flyers stayed up.

Jonah started doubting his decision and if what he was trying to do was a good idea. He even went as far as thinking it was completely idiotic, but being a driven person, he made a pact with himself that he would at least give it a try for the week—Monday, Wednesday, and Friday. If no one came, he could at least say that he gave it a chance.

Jonah stayed away from Liberty Park on Tuesday. He did have a life—sort of—outside of the park. After having lunch with a former coworker, he did some shopping in the afternoon.

On Wednesday, he returned to his bench, but with little hope of any success.

A little after ten o'clock, a man walked hesitantly toward his bench. Jonah watched him with some hesitancy also. He was a Caucasian man who appeared to be in his mid-thirties. His slightly short-length slacks and poorly cut hair, gave him a nerdy appearance. He seemed to be a young professional. Jonah guessed that he was an IT worker or accountant from a local office. The man had an average build, and his hair was slowly letting go up the middle of his head.

"Are you the guy who listens to people?" he said rather loudly from about thirty feet away.

"Yes, I am," Jonah responded not as loudly, "Come on over and have a seat."

The man headed to the other end of the bench. They shook hands and Jonah motioned for him to sit down.

Jonah didn't pretend that the man was first official Fide. "So, I'm guessing you are here to tell me something?"

"Yes," He replied, "How does this work? Do I just start talking?"

This was the same way Pam had started and it was the same way scores of people would start in the future.

"However, you want it to happen," Jonah invited.

"Ok, here I go!" He started.

"A little over a year ago, I went on a field trip with my son's second-grade class. We rode busses up Millcreek Canyon where the class was going to take a hike of about two hours. Two classes were going on the trip. Since there were almost sixty kids, we broke up into groups of six to eight kids so that it wouldn't just be one solid cluster of kids going up together. The groups were spaced about five minutes apart. Mine was the last. I had seven kids including my son."

The man stopped for a second to make sure Jonah was still listening. The Listener looked the man in the eyes to show that he was.

He continued, "the hike was easy at first, then rose into the mountains a little steeper, but still manageable for the students. The morning started clear and pretty chilly for a late spring day. We had all prepared well with windbreakers and other light jackets. After about an hour on the trail, the wind started to pick up. The sound of the wind rustling through the trees concerned a few of the kids, but I calmed them by saying it was normal. The kids were also solaced by one of their classmates, Sofia Martinez—who's family had done the same hike the previous week. She assured them that this hike was the same as the previous week with her family.

"The winds became wet and soon a cold stinging rain was hitting us in the face. As you could imagine, this wasn't popular with the kids. No one was crying, but they were clearly distressed.

"Either no one had checked the weather beforehand, or this was a freak late spring storm which can certainly happen here in the mountains.

"As I assessed the situation, I realized we were probably closer to the end than the beginning of the trail, so we trudged on. The cold rain soon turned to sleet, then snow. My group of kids bunched closely around me looking much as when kids played soccer at that age.

"By this time some were crying, but surprisingly levelheaded as we started our descent. A few times the snow created a complete white-out and we could barely see the trail in front of us. Gradually, Sofia worked her way to the front of the group. Whether to impress her friends or she truly felt confident in her hiking prowess, she started leading the group while I remained generally in the back to make sure we didn't lose anyone.

"What I didn't know, about this time down by the busses, search and rescue teams were being dispatched. All but two groups had made it back to the busses. Soon, the other group made it back and all eyes were on the wall of snow looking for us.

"Sofia continued looking at the ground and trail ahead assuring us that she remembered this part and we were still on the trail."

On the bench, Jonah realized he was actually sitting on the edge listening to the man's telling of the tale. He was intrigued by the man's story.

The man continued, "What seemed an eternity, Sofia eventually led us out and we emerged from the trees. The flashing lights of the emergency vehicles glowed through the fog and blew snow before us.

"We were greeted by first responders with blankets. The kids in the busses were cheering. Teachers hugged the kids and got them to the warmth of the bus.

"The emergency workers assessed all our conditions. The teachers came to me quickly and gave me hugs and thanked me for saving all the kids. Apparently, the scene at the busses had been one of desperation and low hope. They worried it could've ended tragically.

"I heard more than one person refer to me as a hero. In reality, Sofia was the hero. I had no doubt that it could've ended catastrophically had it not been for that seven-year-old girl.

"When I finally got on the bus, the kids were cheering, and my son was telling everyone I was a hero. He looked so proud as his friends patted him on the back."

The man stopped and took a break from his story. This often happened as Fides got to the climax of their story.

He continued, "a few days later, I was honored at a school assembly in the gym. All my group sat up front, including Sofia. I don't think she ever realized that she was the actual hero. She cheered for me along with everyone else. You can probably tell by now; my shame is that I never corrected anyone and told them about Sofia. I kept all the credit for myself. Because my son was so proud, I didn't want to take that away from him.

"That's the disgrace I carry with me. It's too late or I'm too weak to correct it. Until this day, they think I'm some hero, but I'm not. I've decided I can never tell anyone and will carry this guilt with me for a long, long time."

The man completed his story. He appeared ashamed to look directly at Jonah. He kept his head down.

Jonah interrupted his silence. "Do you feel better about telling me?"

"I feel embarrassed right now. It's a hard thing to admit."

Jonah comforted him. "It's not my place to judge. My bench is a judgment-free zone. I would tell you that your misstep could've been much worse. Here on the bench, I hear quite a variety of stories." Again, he was pretending that he had been doing this for a long time. The man didn't know he was the first official Fide.

He seemed comforted. Not wanting to linger, he thanked me for the time and confirmed that the conversation was confidential.

As he walked away, he seemed to hold his head a little higher, but not much. Jonah hoped that his telling the story would get him well on his way to healing.

Walking away, the man passed a girl in her twenties who appeared to want to speak with the listener on the bench. Apparently, the flyer was working, and Jonah's new mission had begun to take shape.

As the girl walked toward him, Jonah couldn't help but remember a similar girl who first caught his eye during the first weeks of his new position at the opening of the new store in Midvale. That had been almost thirty-five years earlier.

Chapter 6

Love at First Sight Takes Time

Sometimes love at first sight can take a while.

The Wasatch Mountains began their life about twelve million years ago. In the time since, the melting snow has created small streams, which, along with the wind and rain, have delicately shaped the valleys and crevices into their current majestic existence.

To Jonah, the time for the mountains' creation seemed about the same as the time it took to win the girl's affection.

The first time Jonah saw Michelle was on the second day of new employee orientation at the opening of the store. As the new Assistant

Manager, he wasn't involved directly in the employee training and when he was brought in, he was relegated to a camp chair set up in the front and off to the side of the group. Initial training was left to the Department Managers. On the first day, he was asked to introduce himself to the newbies. In a make-shift classroom in the middle of the camping department, He stood in front of the fifty new employees and told them how great a place Mountain Impact Sporting Goods was to work. As confident as Jonah was in his knowledge of outdoor equipment, he wasn't very poised in front of groups. As he stood and tentatively moved to the front of the group, it was difficult to imagine that the young man was so confident in himself and his abilities. His introduction took only two minutes, although other introductions had taken much longer. After his awkward speech, he stood at the back and learned from the example of store manager, Andy Christenson, who took thirty minutes to go over the expectations from the management.

Andy had been transferred from another store in Salt Lake. In Jonah's few weeks of getting ready for the opening, he had quickly grown to admire Andy. Even though Andy was much older than Jonah, they related well. He had a wife and two teenage girls. He had grown up in

Jackson Hole, Wyoming enjoying the outdoor offerings of the Grand Tetons and Yellowstone National Parks. Andy was in his early forties with a close-cut head of blonde hair. He had kept himself in shape during the years and was known as an avid skier.

Jonah stood with his hands clasped in front of him, fingers interlocking. As he did so, he listened to Andy's unrehearsed, but confident delivery and admired it. Jonah had always been goal-oriented, and at that moment, made being better at public speaking one of his goals.

As he listened and learned from Andy, he surveyed the new recruits. The new workers were as diverse as the population in general. Most were between twenty and thirty years old. The few older employees were taking notes on legal pads or ringed pocket notepads. The couple of high school-aged kids were trying hard to stay engaged. They reminded Jonah of the time when he first worked for the company in Boulder. He wondered how many of them would end up making a career of this job although they had no intention of it at this time.

He first noticed Michelle as the group was taking a short stretch break. She didn't see him, so he gazed for a little bit too long unnoticed.

She appeared to be about his age but seemed much more advanced socially. Michelle carried herself with much grace and confidence. He thought that confidence bordered on the edge of cockiness. Her brunette hair was pulled back in a ponytail giving her a tomboyish feel. Pulling her hair back revealed a very pretty face with high cheekbones and full lips. She appeared to wear no makeup; either because she didn't need to or didn't feel the obligation to do so for this job. She emitted a natural glow. Jonah wasn't close enough to know for sure but guessed she was about five feet eight, a couple of inches shorter than himself.

From what Jonah could surmise from this distance, she had a very athletic body. She wore khaki shorts and an R.E.M. t-shirt even though outside it was the waning part of winter and the weather still had a bite to it. He could tell she had the lean structure of a swimmer or a runner—a beautiful, striated gazelle. He decided his analysis of Michelle was bordering on creepy, so he stopped the examination before she caught his eye from across the room.

It was almost a week after the store opened when he saw her again. She was stocking hiking boots during one of the grand opening sales.

Not wanting to look as though he was stalking her—which he sort of was—he introduced himself first to one of her coworkers.

Jonah then turned to Michelle and repeated what he had said to the other worker, "Hi, I'm Jonah Freeman, the Assistant Manager for the store."

"I know, I heard what you said to her," she said without even stopping to look at him, "I'm Michelle Bohnan," she continued briefly as she continued stocking the boots.

He continued with the forced conversation anyway. "How do you enjoy working here so far, Michelle?"

"To tell you the truth, this is only my third shift. I go to school full-time." She answered, still without giving him the decency of eye contact.

"I see. What are you studying?" he inquired.

She finally, looked at him. For the first time, Jonah could see her piercing hazel eyes. From this close, she was stunning. "Look. If you don't mind, Tim—the Department Manager—told me I had to get this stocking done before I could leave, so I really don't have time to talk."

At that point, Jonah learned a life lesson; his title did not automatically give him the respect he thought inevitably came with it.

"Oh, ok. Well, we can talk later," he said walking away and feeling slightly chastised.

His next interaction with her was in the break room about a week later. He approached her cautiously. "Well, you're not stocking boots now, are you up for a chat?"

She looked up at him while chewing a granola bar. Michelle guessed his interest in her was more than a manager's and assumed he was awkwardly hitting on her. Without saying anything, she cleared her backpack from the chair next to her and pointed to the now empty seat.

He simply said, "thanks," and sat in the chair, straightening it as he sat down.

"What did you want to know?" she asked. This time she seemed less put off but still not overly welcoming.

"Oh, I'm just trying to get to know everyone. It helps work seem a little more fun," he said with all the Assistant Managerness he could muster.

Michelle certainly thought Jonah was attractive. He was an athletic black man with short hair. He wore clean pressed Dockers and a long-sleeved flannel shirt which were sold in the store. His bright smile contrasted with his warm brown skin.

She was not currently interested in romance.

"Well, I probably won't be here too long, so you don't have to give too much effort getting to know me," she replied. "I'm graduating. from the University of Utah in the summer and will then be moving on."

"That's great," he cautiously proceeded, "what are you studying?"

"Elementary Education. I'm getting my master's degree," she said with a sense of haughtiness, "I hope to teach elementary school and then eventually become a principal."

"Those are great plans." He wanted to tell her that his parents were both professors and both brothers were in top colleges, but then, where did that leave him?

"Well, if you ever need anything, let me know," he said as an escape. She returned to her granola bar and the outdoor magazine she had been reading.

As he walked away, he had the notion that she had probably already forgotten the conversation. She hadn't. She glanced up at him as he walked away, not interested in romance but enjoying the view.

There were other employees to whom he could pay attention, but Jonah couldn't easily get Michelle off his mind.

There were other girls, and he was a young man.

Annie Sorenson was from the Mountain Impact store in Park City. She helped set up the store in preparation for the opening. Annie and Jonah had some immediate banter during those times. They enjoyed joking and occasionally talked about themselves during breaks. Even though she lived in Park City, she wasn't one of the elites who graced the houses near the slopes. Her dad worked for the city and her mom worked as a cashier in a grocery store. Annie wasn't sure what her own future was, but after graduating high school, she started working in the sporting goods store and generally enjoyed it. She was passionate about the outdoors and since she still lived at home, used her employee discount to eat up most of her paycheck.

Annie was not unattractive but had a very earthy, hippy, granola feel that was common amongst the people who worked and shopped at the sporting goods store. Her wavy blonde hair fell to her neck and rested on the top of her shoulders. Annie's face was youthful and cute with just enough freckles to be fun. She certainly wasn't fat, but had a muscular, stout feel about her. A stoutness that could give Jonah a challenge if they ever wrestled. As his dad would say, she was a little rough around the edges. She didn't dress up much. She swore like a factory worker and was generally unrefined, but she was fun, and sometimes fun was all a young adult such as Jonah wanted. He genuinely enjoyed being with her.

They started hanging out regularly when they both closed the store at night. A Wendy's across the street became their rendezvous. Occasionally, he would grab a couple of beers—since she was only 20— and sit on the tailgate of her truck. They enjoyed each other's company enough that when she went back to her home store in Park City, they still made plans to get together a couple of times per week.

It was getting to be late spring at this point, but there were a few ski runs still open, so Annie introduced Jonah to a few of her favorites. Skiing was probably the outdoor activity with which he had the least experience. Immediately, she showed her prowess and left him behind as if he was still on the bunny hill. Over the years ahead, he never gained much expertise on the slopes, but always enjoyed being out in the clean, crisp air.

As their friendship proceeded, things got more serious. They were becoming exclusive in their relationship. They were serious enough that Annie would stay over at Jonah's apartment a night or two per week. Neither of them felt that they wanted to put a label on the relationship, but they knew where they were.

The differences between Jonah and Annie were really in their outlooks on life. With his parents' example, Jonah was raised to set and attain goals. Even though college hadn't worked out for him, it didn't mean he didn't want to chase after dreams and be the best he could be. Annie, on the other hand, was happy living in her parents' house and being a ski bum. Obviously, he thought, people can change, but unless she did, he felt the relationship would have a hard time surviving in the long run. But, in the short run, it was fun.

Store manager, Andy, placed a great deal of emphasis on employee morale. In early summer, an all-employee hike was planned for all the Midvale store employees. Of course, the hike was optional, but all were encouraged to participate and, for managers, it was implied as mandatory. Jonah would've gone anyway. He took any chance to get in the mountains and now that the snow was mostly melted on the trails, he was eager to experience his new playground in the Wasatch Mountains. He wanted to invite Annie, this was totally her type of thing, but Andy wanted the event to just include his store's employees to encourage bonding.

On the morning of the hike, they met at the trailhead halfway up the canyon. The hikers pulled their jackets close to their torsos in this chilly morning air. The smell was rejuvenating, pure as a freshly tilled farm after a rain. The best way to dress for hikes this time of year was to dress in layers—shedding the layers like a stripper in super-slow motion as the day progressed.

Fifteen employees showed up by 7:00 a.m., and they all started the ascent to more than 9,000 feet in elevation. The plan was to hike out and back on different routes ending back at the same trailhead. The estimated time for the hike was four or five hours. The terrain started out tame, the group passed a couple of families with small kids along the way. About an hour in, the trail was tangential to Coyote Lake, a very clear lake with some lily pads collecting on the side near the trail. On this Saturday, the lake was still except for the occasional splash of a rainbow trout breaking the surface of its mountain home. On the opposite side of the lake stood a cow moose drinking amongst the lily pads not paying any attention to the people on the trail. The moose stood in a shaded part of the lake where snow still remained. If the group had watched the moose very long, they would have seen a shy baby moose inch out into the open from behind the protection of its mother.

Most novice hikers stopped at the lake, spent some time fishing or throwing rocks, then returned to their cars. After the lake, the trail got smaller with a much steeper ascent. The group continued up.

As the trail narrowed, the group was forced into a single file for a while. The hike became steep and because the trail on which they hiked was clinging to the side of the mountain on the left, there was a precipitous drop-off on the right. This was nothing unusual for a hike in the mountains, but something of which a hiker had to stay aware.

After half an hour of the steep climb, they came to a small level clearing. The space was at least large enough that they could all gather, retrieve their water bottles, and shed a layer of clothes if they chose. Hikers from other groups passed by on their way up the trail, nodding or exchanging pleasantries as they did.

There was a little small talk amongst the group as they drank, changed, or simply gazed at the beauty of the valley below. Coyote Lake seemed so small below from this vantage point.

The wind was soft, and the air was pure. The slopes of the mountain were mostly quiet except for the wind rushing through the aspens below—where the wind was not so soft.

Suddenly, the hikers were alarmed by a thumping above them to the left. Fifty feet above them, the mountain had released its grip on a small boulder. The group couldn't see it to know how large the boulder was but could all sense from the irregular thumps as it rolled that it was large enough to do damage. All they could do was cover their heads and hope the granite stone would bounce over them.

It didn't.

By the time the boulder was visible, there were only seconds to react. The football-sized rock hit the trail a few feet from Jonah and then bounced directly toward him, too quickly to evade. The bouncing rock appeared it would land by his left foot, but his estimation of the trajectory was wrong. The solid, irregular piece of the mountain hit his leg just above his ankle before it careened over the edge of the trail and on down the mountain through the scrub brush. The sound of the rock lessened until there was a thud a hundred feet below where it found a home.

On the trail, Jonah immediately fell, yanking his knee closely and grasping the point of impact. Over the years, he had learned to deal with accidents out in the wild, so he didn't scream with his pain, but he definitely groaned and writhed for a minute or so on the ground.

Andy had been medically trained while a ski lift operator at Jackson Hole. He quickly knelt beside the injured man and started inspecting the point of impact.

"It doesn't appear to be broken so let me have you stand so I can tell better the extent of any injury." Andy, along with another coworker helped Jonah stand on his right leg leaving the left leg dangling. As he gently pressed around where the rock had assaulted the hiker, Andy surmised it probably didn't break anything. Cautiously and lightly, Jonah put his left foot on the ground. Pain shot through his shin, and he immediately recoiled.

Over the next fifteen minutes or so, he was able to get the foot on the ground and apply a minimal amount of pressure, at least enough to hobble a little.

It was obvious that he couldn't hike anymore and walking back down the trail was questionable.

Anyone trained in emergency response knows that there can't be a lot of emotion instilled into a decision such as this. Options need to be approached with a clear mind.

"Do you want me to have someone run down the trail, find a phone, and call search and rescue?" the manager asked. In the days before cell phones were prevalent, the options were limited.

"Absolutely not!" he responded," I can do it. it will just take some time." The young man was being motivated by his pride and machismo, unnecessarily common in males his age.

Andy turned to the group. "What Jonah really needs is someone to go with him. I know that's not what you came here for, but it's all part of being a team. Is anyone interested in volunteering?"

In just a few seconds, the person who had been holding Jonah up while Andy examined him, volunteered. "Sure, I can do it, no problem."

Randy Judd

Chapter 7

His Serendipitous Rescue

Through the shock of the injury, Jonah hadn't noticed that the one helping hold him up—the volunteer—was Michelle Bohnan.

"Oh no, that's ok," he protested, "I don't want to mess up your hike."

"As I said, it's no problem. I'm definitely strong enough to do it, probably stronger than you!" She grinned as she teased to hopefully take his mind off his pain.

He didn't resist too hard. If he had to be helped by someone, how could he resist a chance to get to know this beauty, even if she would see him in his vulnerable state?

The remainder of the group headed on their way as Michelle helped him hobble slowly down the decline.

After ten minutes and still not out of sight of the clearing, they knew this would be a long trek. The sound of their group ascending diminished until hikers could no longer be heard. It didn't take long for Michelle to understand the reality of the situation. Jonah's pride gave in to letting her actually help him shuffle down the hill. She was right, she was strong, and he found he could rely more and more on her help to relieve his pain.

"I'm sorry, you're having to help me," he said, "I know this isn't the way you had your Saturday planned."

"Unfortunately, I volunteer easily. It's a curse and gets me into trouble sometimes." She smiled.

He was attracted to her smile. Her perfect teeth looked a little too big for her mouth. Even when she didn't smile, her natural resting face offered a hint of that smile.

"I grew up in a family where I am the oldest of six kids. I was responsible for a lot of volunteering, whether I wanted to or not." She laughed slightly.

He responded, "well, I hope you are ok with it this time."

"Yeah, it's all good. Sometimes, you just got to do what you've got to do!"

The couple stopped every thirty minutes or so allowing them to both rest. Jonah felt very lucky they were going downhill all the way to the parking lot so that gravity could assist with the work.

They talked almost nonstop down the trail. The dialog was not rushed or forced, just the natural discussion of who they were.

Michelle had grown up in the Salt Lake City area in a very religious, middle-class family. She had not followed the family's religious beliefs very closely, but she didn't balk at them either. She felt as though the teachings had given her a good moral foundation for her life.

Her dad was a Jr. High Principal and had been the inspiration and role model for Michelle's career plans. Her mom stayed home with the kids during the early years, then returned to school to become a nurse. Michelle's mom had also been an inspiration. Michelle was just finishing up her master's degree in education and already had accepted a teaching position at Neumann Elementary in the nearby town of Granger and she would be teaching fourth graders. She seemed very excited about the new chapter in her life.

Jonah shared his background. Because of her parent's background, he now felt a need to get some credibility by letting her know about his parents' and brothers' intellectual pursuits hoping it would somehow make his undefined position in life look a little better although he wasn't sure how.

They talked a lot about the outdoors: what they enjoyed doing and where they had been. She mostly loved skiing—both downhill and cross-country—and he particularly enjoyed fishing and mountain biking. They both agreed on hiking, fortunately not the kind they were doing at the moment.

Michelle had dated several guys during high school and college but only had a few serious relationships. Most recently, she had just broken up with a boyfriend of two years. This was interesting news to Jonah.

Even though his first assessment of Michelle—during the first few days of the store opening—was that she was somewhat arrogant and aloof, he realized her attitude may have been because that was about the time her last relationship was falling apart. It was undoubtedly weighing heavy on her at that time. Jonah was quick to establish that she was actually quite pleasant in conversation. She not only was open about herself, but she was also skilled in asking questions about him. When she asked a question, she would sincerely listen to the response. Her parents had raised her well and taught her the importance of making another person feel important. Her listening skills were an inspiration to Jonah in his future interactions with others on the bench.

She wanted to know his ambitions in life. Jonah embellished some things in the moment since he wasn't sure how his future would look. It was too embarrassing to disclose that he had no idea. She didn't seem to be condescending about this. Maybe it was because she knew with his family's background, he probably had the genetic makeup to be goal oriented. It could've also been that she was a naturally good person who didn't judge others because of their station in life. Either way, he felt comfortable being with her.

She wasn't wrong about being strong enough to help him. He could feel her muscles react as she supported him over rocks or held him back on steep inclines. Jonah was also aware of her femininity. Her skin was clear and appeared silky soft even on this day when she didn't wear makeup and sweat was meandering down her face. Her hair was again pulled back in a ponytail, revealing some very elegant ears. Her neck was perfect, he thought. As she held him, he was close enough to tell her hair and skin both smelled sweet, even through that morning sweat.

The journey back to the car took about two and a half hours. They stopped by Coyote Lake for an extended rest to let their bodies heal and recover somewhat. The two sat on the grass and lay their heads on their backpacks. Each of them pulled some food from the packs to nourish themselves for the remaining part of the trip.

By now, a half dozen families were playing around the lake. The moose had moved deeper into the woods to avoid the activity. When a Frisbee landed near them, Michelle stood up quickly and threw it back and forth to a couple of kids. It was easy to tell right away that she had an affinity with this age and would make a great teacher and eventually, mother.

After their respite, because the terrain was relatively flat, Jonah decided he could give Michelle a break and limp the rest of the way back by himself. There was a huge part of him that didn't want to so he could remain close to her feminine touch, but he also didn't want her to see him as completely helpless. She graciously accepted his desire for independence. From the edge of the trail, Michelle picked up a thick stick about three feet long, peeled off the smaller twigs, and handed it to him for a walking stick. It gave him the extra support he needed, and he was grateful.

When they finally landed in the parking lot, Jonah left Andy a note under the windshield wiper of his car to let him know they were ok. Jonah thanked Michelle profusely for her help. He wondered how to even thank someone for volunteering for such a monumental task to help someone she barely knew.

"I owe you a huge dinner!" he offered, "do you eat steak?"

"Of course, who doesn't? But you don't owe me anything. I was just helping someone who needed my help," she replied.

"Have you ever eaten at Alpine Steakhouse at the mouth of the Canyon?" He asked knowing all the time that he wouldn't order ribs or wear khaki pants.

"No, but that sounds wonderful. For now, let's get you to an urgent care and get that leg looked at."

he protested. "Oh, you don't need to come. Because it's my left foot, I can still drive fine. You've done more than enough already." Selling his Jeep CJ a few months earlier had been hard, but now the thought of clutching the manual transmission made him cringe. He was happy his new truck was an automatic.

"Nonsense," she said, "what kind of friend would I be if I didn't see this through?"

The word 'friend' eased out of her mouth and landed in his soul. Jonah had had many friends in his life but felt more honored to be hers.

Michelle trailed in her Subaru. After a fifteen-minute drive to the clinic, Michelle once again pulled his arm over her head and let his weight rest on her. As a new friend, she waited with the Highlights and Sports Illustrated while in another room, the doctor diagnosed Jonah sitting on an exam table with crinkly butcher paper beneath him.

Luckily, nothing was broken. The doctor said the injury appeared to be a deep bruise with no muscle or ligament damage. She told him to use crutches for a couple of weeks. He agreed, knowing he wouldn't. As Jonah exited the exam room, he found her warm smile waiting. Her presence stirred his being and not just in a hormonal manner but in his soul.

"Let me buy you lunch. It's the least I can do," Jonah insisted.

Across the busy street in front of the clinic was a small coffee shop situated in front of a strip mall. Crossing the busy street was reminiscent of playing Frogger during their childhoods. The strip mall was deteriorating, but the coffee shop was modern with a slanted roof and earth tone exterior. They had a complete choice of seating and settled into a corner table. It was mid-afternoon, and if not for the Indie music playing overhead, the couple's voices would've bounced off the cement floor and plaster walls until even the barista could've understood every word.

Their interaction was easy. During the last six hours, they had been enrolled in a crash course of getting to know each other that normally would've taken several dates. The couple traded tales about their families, childhood, and outdoor adventures (Jonah always led with his telling of the beach, crabs, and tide in California). As she shared her life stories, Jonah watched her eyes and lived the experiences shared across her lips.

"I've got to tell you, Jonah, the thing I'm most surprised by you is your confidence. You're almost cocky. but humble, if that makes sense. I guess I'd label it *Humble Cockiness!*" She quipped, "I mean, not to be disrespectful, but you don't have any college education. You seem to be trying to find your way in life. Yet, anyone can look at you and have a feeling you WILL be successful in all you do. What gives you such confidence?"

Jonah thought a few seconds and then replied, "if that's true, I would have to give credit to my mom and her parenting style. Mom didn't spend a lot of time trying to build my self-esteem by telling me I was 'Special'. Instead, she gave me opportunities to accomplish small tasks— and later bigger tasks—so that I could build my self-esteem without being told by outside voices. She knew, that being black, I would probably have a difficult time in some aspects of life, and she wanted to give me the power to overcome those struggles. Her process gave me the strength to ignore the voices trying to put me down in life. My self-worth doesn't come from the outside; it comes from the inside. I get tired of people in life who don't seem to care about others—holding open doors, common courtesies, not following rules, and so on—

because their mommies told them they were special. All of us are special and yet none of us is special. We all have strengths and weaknesses. I guess my mom's style of teaching is what really shaped my confidence and made me who I am. "

"That's profound, Jonah! And a wonderful tribute to your mom. It just goes to show that I am right in my assessment that you do have your head on straight."

Jonah replied, "Thanks, Michelle. And by the way, I guess I would prefer to call it *Cocky Humbleness.*"

She reacted with a soft smile.

As they rose to leave, Jonah strolled over to the counter and dropped a few dollars in the tip jar. He second-guessed his action wondering if it appeared garish. Michelle simply construed it as considerate.

After exiting the cafe, they approached their cars. Michelle philosophically interjected, "Isn't it interesting that this morning when we woke up, we had no idea that we would get to know each other so well and spend so much time together. I enjoyed the day with you, Jonah."

Jonah simply replied, "Me too."

He wanted to thank that football-sized rock resting somewhere in the scrub brush of the mountains.

That night, Jonah was supposed to go on a date with Annie, but he called to recount to her the day's events, being careful how much he talked about Michelle. Annie had previously shown her jealous side when she walked into a stockroom and saw that he was working beside one of the female employees.

Annie certainly understood not getting together but did ask temptingly if she could help in any way. Jonah declined her offer because he felt quite content at the moment.

Michelle ended her employment at Mountain Impact soon after her experience with Jonah. She was putting the final touches on her new teaching position and needed to apply all her energy to making perfect her introduction to her profession. The two spoke often on the phone and met once a week for coffee or lunch. On one call, Jonah mentioned that he had yet to take her for the steak reward as promised. They set a time to do that.

He picked her up on a Thursday. Walking to the door of her apartment, the event felt as though it was an official date although they hadn't approached it as such. She shared her apartment with a couple of roommates from school. When she came to the door, she flashed that great smile. She looked even better than he remembered. She had applied a little makeup for the evening. She had beautiful skin without makeup, but the makeup took a well-sculptured piece of marble and polished it. Jonah found it difficult not to stare at her. She wore jeans and a new white t-shirt which was tight enough to give her a more formal look than an oversized t-shirt would've given, but not so tight as to look stifling. The shirt was certainly tight enough to get the boy's attention. Her hair, which was normally in a ponytail, now rested playfully on her shoulders. As they walked toward his truck, he resisted opening the door for her, still unsure of the date status or even if she was the type of woman who would want the door opened for her.

The other times they had gotten together recently were more as two friends meeting in the middle of the day, but this seemed more deliberate. Both found the evening a little awkward, unsure of what this night was.

The pitch of his truck tires lowered as they slowed to enter the parking lot of the steakhouse. The parking lot of gravel popped underneath the tires until they came to a stop.

As the hostess seated them, Michelle thanked the hostess. After getting settled, Jonah noticed that Michelle rested her forearms on the edge of linen covered table making sure not to lay her elbows on the table itself. A few minutes later after initial small talk and ordering, she delicately placed her linen napkin on her lap. Even though she behaved as a tomboy in other circumstances, she had been taught by her parents how to carry herself properly in these circumstances. Jonah followed suit and Michelle recognized that his professor parents had taught him etiquette also. As she said please and thank you to the wait staff and busboys, Jonah appreciated this having often been treated as a servant himself.

Their steaks were grilled perfectly, hot and sizzling on the plate. The couple meandered their way through the courses, not wanting to rush. As the tables around them emptied, not to be re-sat, they found themselves on an island at the edge of the dining room. They quickly melted into their own world with only an occasional interruption from someone refilling drinks or clearing dishes. The couple spent time in real dialog, giving and taking. The dialog was mostly lighthearted with an occasional serious moment interrupting the banter.

Normally, Michelle would've been uncomfortable taking so much time at the table knowing that the server could get more tips by turning the table. Tonight, though, the tables were staying empty. Wanting to converse as long as they could, they decided to leave a larger tip as a reward for their lingering.

As the crowd dwindled and the chairs started to be flipped up on the tables, they rose to leave. A glance at her phone surprised Michelle that they had been there for over three hours. Approaching the truck, Jonah opened her door for her this time. It seemed natural since he had to unlock it anyway, but he did enjoy being chivalrous.

The twenty minutes back to her apartment arrived too quickly. After putting the transmission in park and turning off the engine, neither one made a move to end the night. The couple sat for another thirty minutes still talking. The calming night sounds of nearby birds and far-off traffic floated through the dry evening air and drifted in through the open windows.

Michelle knew what she wanted and was getting impatient waiting. She leaned in and kissed him. He couldn't remember ever having a girl initiate a kiss with him. Even better than the steaks, her kiss was delectable. She lingered in her kiss long enough so there would be the anticipation for the future when the affection could be a larger part of the date. It was just as a first kiss should be. The moment shouldn't be wasted on the dance floor of a club with someone just met but should be a delicate event that one can look back on with tenderness.

"I really had fun tonight, Jonah. Let's do this again soon."

"I'd love to," he said, his face still flush.

With this short exchange, she got out of the truck. Jonah watched with interest as she walked to her door. Michelle turned before reaching for the doorknob and waved. He viewed her with delight as she ascended the stairs and went inside.

Soon after, things went from heaven to hell for Jonah.

When he arrived at his apartment, he could see the streetlight glowing on the top of Annie's car in front. As he approached—and before she had seen him —he could see she was frantically throwing items onto the sidewalk. When he got close enough, Jonah could see that the things she was throwing were possessions of his that had been at her house or in her car: clothes, CDs, toiletries, and so forth.

Annie wasn't making any sound in her tantrum until she saw him. When she did, she picked up some of the things she had already discarded and fired them at him. A Green Day CD struck him in the temple. As if awakened out of some profanity-free sleep, she started lashing out with a string of expletives. When he heard the word *Skank*, for the first time he realized that she had heard about Michelle through the *Mountain Impact* grapevine, and she wasn't going to give him a chance to explain.

While still ranting, she went to her driver's side door and pulled out a hunting knife! Every good outdoorsman keeps a knife, but they're usually not used as a weapon. Jonah kept on the opposite side of the car as she circled quickly but randomly. He had no trouble staying away from her.

He was more embarrassed than fearful at the scene. Many neighbors were watching from their porches or behind pulled blinds. He felt lucky that someone had called the police. When they pulled up, He was relieved.

At least he *WAS* relieved until they quickly approached, with guns drawn, and ordered Jonah to the ground. One officer handcuffed him, put him in the back of his car, and proceeded to question Annie as the victim.

Fortunately, many of the witnesses came to his defense, and eventually, the police released him without even an apology. He didn't know why he would expect otherwise.

Jonah and Annie's relationship was over. This currently left only one lucky young lady in his sites. He wasn't sure if Michelle understood that yet, but he was going to do his best to show her.

Jonah waited a few days to call Michelle again, he didn't want to seem too eager. As inexperienced at love, as he was, he at least thought that was the right move.

Knowing how active she was, it was only appropriate that their next date was something adventurous. After talking on the phone every couple of days and meeting once for a smoothie, he waited until his ankle was sufficiently healed to ask her on a real date. Jonah invited her to spend the majority of Sunday mountain biking with him up the canyon. She eagerly accepted.

Summer was now completely showing its full colors. Even though the temperature in the Salt Lake Valley was sweltering, the cool moist air of Big Cottonwood Canyon would be a retreat to natural air conditioning. With both bikes riding in the back of his truck, they unloaded them at the trailhead. Although they knew the mountains would offer solitude, the ten cars in the parking lot assured them they were not completely alone.

"It's too bad we couldn't come up on a weekday, so we could have the mountain to ourselves," Michelle said.

"Stupid jobs," Jonah responded with a playful grin.

The wildflowers before them were a carpet of color against the majestic backdrop of snowcapped mountains. At the trailhead, they were hidden from the main road. Except for the traffic on the canyon's road and the buzz of a large fly circling them, the morning was restful and silent. The trail welcomed them with a meadow of tall grass. The unfriendly grass lashed their legs as they rode through. After a half mile of terrain as flat and easy as any city street, nature began offering her challenges and made them work for their fun.

Their muscles were strained as the cyclists ascended many of the hills of soil and rock. Although they were both more fit than many their age, their strength was still challenged as they pumped up the trail. These strenuous efforts were always rewarded by a descent allowing them to catch their breath and enjoy the cool mountain air chilling the sweat as it whipped across their faces and through their hair.

After two hours of continually climbing and then plunging, they stopped for lunch. On a gently sloping granite rock face, they rested with their packs. Their vantage point overlooked the canyon below while also providing a vista of the mountain range above them. High on the wind above, a hawk glided with little energy as the graceful predator searched for unsuspecting prey on which to swoop. Occasionally, other cyclists passed by with a quick greeting or a head nod.

On the edge of a clearing fifty feet away, a coyote made an unexpected midday appearance. Michelle quietly pointed it out to Jonah in a whisper so as to not startle the animal. Soon, it saw the humans and quietly leaped into the underbrush.

"Do you know what's intriguing about coyotes?" Michelle asked and then answered. "They are one of the most loyal mates in the animal world. They rarely stray from one lifetime mate. I look forward to being a coyote in my own right someday."

Not subtle, she was making a preemptive statement about her feelings toward monogamy. If that was her purpose, he agreed.

Michelle spread a cloth on the exposed rock and began unpacking the meal she had volunteered to bring. Her mom had provided homemade bread. It was easy to imagine the smell of her mom's kitchen as the bread was being baked. Sliced lunch meat took its honored place on the bread. Freshly cut carrots and celery sticks rounded out the lunch, meant to nourish but not bog them down. Each of them leaned back on their elbows and had an apple for dessert. The meal was satisfying and so was the camaraderie. The conversation meandered wherever the dialogue took it. Talk was sometimes serious, sometimes light, but always natural and easy. They were surprised when they realized the thirty-minute stop for lunch had instantly become two hours. The time had sprinted by. They both commented on how they enjoyed the talking, the banter, and just being together. Jonah and Michelle knew they were friends, but it was becoming obvious to both that they were getting closer than either of them had expected in such a short time.

Because they were both young and had remained fit, most of their time together involved athletic activities to challenge each other. Michelle was extremely competitive. She could be a sore loser, but she could also be a sore winner.

With the sun beating down on the green concrete of the court, the two athletes chose their sides. On the near side of the net, Michelle removed her outer clothing to reveal her shorts and tank top. Jonah immediately took notice. She unzipped the racquet-shaped cover and pulled the grip until the expensive racquet was taken from its protection. From the side pocket of her bag, she removed a Pringles-like can and opened it. Three yellow spheres fell on the hard surface. Each bounced in its own direction. ready to fulfill its purpose.

On the far side, Jonah stretched and jumped readying himself for the match. The two gladiators had parity on the court, and they took the competition seriously.

The Listening Bench

After a grueling two-hour match, they found themselves at match point. The sun blasted directly above causing Michelle's skin to be flush and wet. The perspiration caused her tank top to cling to her as skin. Jonah's black cropped hair glistened as sweat trailed down his face resembling tears. They were both intent on winning, and neither of them backed down to be defeated. Michelle was serving and had the advantage. After faulting on her first attempt, she nailed the second serve, and it sailed past his outreached racquet.

She celebrated the point with a taunting scream! Michelle, dripping in sweat, threw her Donnay racquet like a Frisbee into the net. She then fell to her knees, threw her head back, and clenched her fist.

"YES! …YES!," She screamed orgasmically.

Jonah—not immediately congratulatory—walked to his bag and dabbed his sweat. The vanquished warrior made his way to her side of the net humbled.

They never took each other's exuberance personally. They were always supportive of each other's accomplishments, both in sports and in life.

By the time Michelle started teaching school in the fall, the couple had been dating for a couple of months. Even though they hadn't labeled their relationship, their status was obvious to both.

"Well," she said one night after a date as he dropped her off at her apartment, "My parents want me to invite you to dinner this Sunday. Are you ready to meet the parents?"

"I could handle a good home-cooked meal. I haven't had one in quite a while," he responded. "Are YOU ready for it? I do usually clean up pretty well for the adults. Have you warned them?"

She replied as if she didn't know what he was talking about, "You mean that you're a brat?"

"I mean because I'm black."

"Of course, I know what you mean. Yeah, it came up not long after I told them about the hike. They were surprised a little a first, but I doubt they will have a problem with it. If they do, then I will have a problem with THEM."

The fact that Jonah was African American had been a reason for consternation whenever he met someone new, especially the all-white family of his girlfriend.

Chapter 8

Babysitter Fide

At the bench at Liberty Park, Jonah found early that what the Fides wanted to tell was seldom a happy tale as most of them were coming to him because of a weight they were carrying and of which they wanted to rid themselves. As another day began, people started to arrange themselves at the listening bench. Jonah casually peered across the grass at them, not staring as to make them self-conscious. The people on his bench were varied in race, gender, and age, but unified by their need to share a wound or other secret. Jonah sometimes worried about the overall impact their stories would have on him over time. He thought of a police friend of his who finally had to retire after the daily pounding of sad situations she dealt with day after day. By reflecting on the good he was doing and the lift in their spirits when they left, he was able to keep positive.

A rhythm was setting in on the bench and the routine was good. Every day Fides came to his lakeside confessional to cleanse their souls of things they could not reveal to others.

On a late spring morning, after the frost had disappeared until another day, the first person Jonah welcomed was a man walking briskly toward him. He confirmed that Jonah was the man from the flyer. After his verification, He was invited to sit down and talk which he did with a bounce.

The vibrant man was in his late thirties or even early forties if he had taken good care of himself. His salon-styled brown hair had hints of blond streaked throughout. The man's attire was reminiscent of GQ and his nails were manicured flawlessly. After the initial preamble, he started his story.

"I had something happen to me as a teenager which I've never been able to shake," he started.

"As a young person, I was asked to babysit two pre-teen girls in our neighborhood. By today's standards, that just seems weird. Our family was friends with theirs, so the parents knew me well. The girls were safe with me, and the family assumed so.

"I started babysitting on a regular basis, once per week or so. They paid well and I could do homework after the girls went to sleep. After a few months of watching them, suddenly the invitations to babysit stopped. I didn't think much about it when it had only been a week or two since I last tended them, but when the weeks turned to months, I was curious what I might have done to offend the parents. I recollected my interactions with the parents and the girls and couldn't think of anything I may have done.

"It wasn't until years later as an adult that I suddenly had a heavy thought emerge. What if I had done something that could've been misconstrued as inappropriate affection with the girls?

"You see, I'm gay. I've known from a very early age that I was different from my friends and by the time I was eleven or twelve, knew I was gay. I didn't tell most people for several years.

"I would've had no desire to touch them inappropriately, but I've always been affectionate with everybody. I did hug them and read them stories while they sat on my lap and such. I've wondered if they told the parents and the parents stopped letting me babysit just to be safe. Now, being a dad myself, I can totally see their point of view and how what I was doing was not ok."

The man's rapid-fire telling of the story had an urgency to arrive at the end.

"This all has been in the back of my mind since I realized that there may have been a problem. A few years ago, I thought about the girls' memory of the events. I thought about reaching out to them and explaining to them I never intended anything unsuitable. I've decided against it so far for these reasons: If they remember and it had been an issue, bringing it up now may bring up old feelings that may have healed. I could be that guy that they have been telling their therapist about for years. If they don't remember anything, I may plant ideas in their heads that may cause them to need a therapist.

"Either way, I could really mess with their psychological wellbeing. There is not a winning choice."

"So, I just pray that the events didn't cause any pain for them, but I'm not going to reach out."

His eyes looked inward as he was formulating his conclusion.

"I just needed to tell someone, maybe the cosmos, that I didn't do anything to those girls. I just hope if they think I did, they are able to move on, but I didn't do anything requiring me to forgive myself."

This pause let Jonah know that the man was through. It had been one of his shorter sessions. The man sat looking impatiently at Jonah as if he was waiting for his reaction or advice. After all, he had just revealed to the listener something very personal.

Jonah broke the silence, "Thank you for sharing that with me today. I'm hoping by telling me, it served the purpose that you came to me here today."

"Do you have any advice for me?" He asked.

Jonah replied, "No, I really don't. I typically don't give advice and your question is much more complicated than I'm trained to help with. Have you gone to a therapist? If not, you may consider that."

He breathed a quick sigh, signaling his perturbation at Jonah's response, Jonah hoped he understood.

Jonah finished, "Did telling me help, though?"

"Yes, you're the first person I've ever told. It feels good to get it out there even if there are no correct answers."

After thanking the listener, he stood up and exited as quickly as he had entered.

Quite often, people would come to the bench, not for confession, but simply because they were lonely. Jonah received many sad stories from people who were walking in the park alone every day simply because they had no one to talk with. Some had no friends, no family, and no connections at all. These wrenched his heart. In the beginning, He felt they didn't meet the purpose of his bench, but he couldn't turn them away. In these sessions, he would ask more questions and give them genuine conversation. In these instances, his *Listening Bench* became more of a *Friend Bench*. Jonah had the inspiration that at some point, he should figure out a way to serve these people also. Maybe named *The Conversation Bench* so any two people could meet and talk for a certain amount of time.

He put the idea on the back burner for a while. Presently, he had plenty of people who just want to tell him some secret.

As he continued with his mission, Jonah had no idea an upcoming event would make a difference in people's lives for years to come.

For now, he was caught up in the memory of his first meeting of Michelle's family and being raised a black man in a generally white man's world.

Randy Judd

Chapter 9

On Being Black

With Phillis York Freeman, almost everything was directed. Very little happened by chance. It was the same with how her family dealt with their heritage.

Phillis York had been raised in Little Rock, Arkansas. She grew up in an all-black neighborhood near Central High School which she wasn't allowed to attend. It would still be a few years after she graduated high school that Central High would be one of the first integrated schools in the country—assisted by the National Guard. She sometimes talked to her family about the ugly things she had seen growing up. Somewhere along the way, she decided the best way out of her circumstances and the most forceful way to prove others' prejudices wrong was to continue her education as far as she could and become the best person she could be.

How she had been treated growing up was the motivating factor for her to attend college. She attained her bachelor's degree at the University of Arkansas. She continued her education through scholarships and earned her master's and doctorate at the University of Texas in Austin. Phillis York was one of the first African American women to get a Ph.D. in Texas.

In determining the next steps, she visited a relative who worked at Tuskegee Institute in Alabama. Phillis was immediately captivated by such a place. As she strolled the campus, she was surrounded by black professionals with masters, doctorates. None of the individuals had to prove themselves more than others. They were all respected for their individual achievements alone. After several days on campus and after meeting with several department heads, she was offered a research position in the Department of Business.

Phillis was honored and knew she could feel fulfilled and challenged in this environment.

The evening of the offer, Phillis called her fiancé, Abel Freeman. They had met through her cousin who served in Korea with Abel.

On the call, she explained her experience over the last couple of days at the institute. He listened intently.

"I just believe this would be a great place to raise a family away from all the ugliness you and I see every day," she said.

He responded, "I see what you mean, it must be an amazing environment, but let me ask you a question. After our children are grown, will they continue to live in that all-black world? Will they learn the skills they need to overcome the bigotries they will have in a white man's world? Conversely, will they have the chance to experience good people of other races? Or will their cocoon eventually hurt them?"

She pondered the question, then answered, "You make a really good point, Abel. I guess on some level I was feeling those same things but had never put feelings into words."

She applied for and accepted a teaching position at the University of Colorado even though she was well aware of the lack of diversity on the campus. Being ever fearless, Dr. Freeman moved forward to become one of the first black professors on campus.

Abel Freeman had come to the University after serving in the US Army during the Korean War. Being a member of the Army had a way of taking away some of the bias and bigotry that he had experienced growing up black in Kansas. When a soldier is part of an infantry unit, they didn't care about the color of the soldier's skin in the next foxhole, only that he was a good shot.

Over the years before they had children, Phyllis and Abel engaged in many discussions on the subject of race. By the time their sons were born, their family's culture toward race was very much decided.

The Freeman boys were taught to hold their heads high and be proud of their African American roots. As teenagers, each boy was sent to stay with some of their cousins in Arkansas for a week during the summer. This was done so that they could not only stay connected to their relatives but also so they could be exposed to a larger black experience.

The boys were also taught that if they were going to be successful, they had to try a little harder than others around them. People may expect less of them so the only way to be equal was to be better.

They were warned how to act if pulled over by police; put your keys on the dash, hands on the steering wheel, and explain all your movements. They always remembered this when it was necessary, and they were stopped many times over the years. These experiences prepared him for the night of Annie's explosive scene when he was found himself seated in the back of the patrol car.

One of Abel's favorite stories to tell happened when he had been teaching at the university for about a year. He had decided to go into his office very early one morning to grade papers. A police car followed him into the parking lot and the officer—who didn't know Abel—asked, "What are you doing here this early in the morning?"

"I'm here to visit Professor Freeman's office."

"Well, I don't think anyone is going to be up there yet, why don't we just go up together?"

Abel agreed. He couldn't help but think toying with the officer would be fun.

Nothing was said as they climbed the stairs to the second floor. There was an elevator, but the cop was overweight, so Abel chose the stairs instead. As they got to the door of the second-story office, the officer said through labored breaths, "Here's his office and no one is here, what have you got to say for yourself now?"

Reaching deep into his trouser pocket, saying nothing, Abel pulled his key chain out. As he discovered the correct key, he aimed it toward the lock.

"How do you have a key? Where did you get it?"

The black professor replied with all the dignity he could muster, "They gave it to me when I was hired. I'm Professor Freeman and this is my office."

Humiliated, the large man huffed and without responding further to Abel, pivoted on the heels of his black regulation leather boots and stormed away. He approached the elevator and pushed the down button several times in quick succession. His crimson face disappeared behind shutting doors.

The Freeman parents taught the boys to be polite, well-mannered, poised, and respectful. They weren't allowed to follow the urban or African American trends of their cousins in the south. They were expected to remain conservative in their hairstyles and attire.

Looking back, Jonah felt that they were pretty much being raised to be white. He didn't blame his parents too much. He felt they were trying to do the best they knew how. Right or wrong, they thought the best way to be successful in a white man's world was to act as a white man.

One of Abel's favorite sayings was *the best way to combat other people's prejudice is to not do the things that their prejudice says you will do. If you do those things, it just validates their bigotry.'*

Jonah actually reveled in standing out in high school. It was part of his outgoing personality. He reveled in being special. There was only a half dozen black kids in his school. He was friends with all of them but had many more white friends. Jonah was aware early that there were different expectations put on him than his friends. He had to worry about driving in nice neighborhoods when going to visit a friend. When he was in a group where something happened that shouldn't have, he knew he would probably be singled out for accusations. He was lucky that his friends—and even the adults in his world—knew him well enough to stand up for him if there were suspicions.

Jonah only dated white girls partly because there was practically none of his race in his town. His dating of Sarah was seen as appalling by some school rednecks, but the rest of the school was very supportive.

Sometimes, Jonah couldn't help but feel he betrayed his race. With all the African American issues during the years, he never was an activist or protested. He just felt sorry that others didn't have the life he was afforded.

When he moved to Utah, there were even fewer people of color, but using the things his parents taught him, he was able to handle himself in most situations where color was an issue. When in public places, Jonah noticed a cultural nod between black individuals he met passing in the mall. It was their way of saying, 'I feel you, brother'.

He was always apprehensive to meet the family of someone he was dating.

He was becoming increasingly enamored by Michelle, so he particularly wanted the upcoming interaction to go well.

Chapter 10

Courtship

After all the anxiety —mostly for Michelle— around meeting her family, it was a very nice event.

Michelle's family, a close, religious family with five kids of which she was the oldest, welcomed Jonah into their home with open arms. Jonah wondered if they had a family meeting about going overboard to make the black man feel welcome. He did feel welcome, and their actions felt very genuine. He ended up having a two-hour conversation with her dad. They talked about fishing, sports, and life in general. Jonah knew he was on stage, not only because he was the new boyfriend, but because he was the new African American boyfriend.

Jonah played a pickup game of basketball with her little brothers. Basketball was never his strong sport, but he held his own over the fifteen-year-old. As he left, Michelle's mom loaded his arms with Tupperware full of meals for the next few days.

"Well, what do you think?" Michelle quizzed.

"They were great. I really had fun and hope they were fine with me."

"I have no doubt they approved. I could see it in the way they interacted with you. They are pretty genuine people. They don't hide their feelings easily."

"I'm happy to hear that."

◆ ◆ ◆

Anyone over a certain age will agree that time seems to accelerate as life moves along. To a child, years click as a roller coaster gradually climbing the first hill. The clicks act as guideposts such as birthdays, the start of school, the end of school, or Christmas. Into the twenties as the car crests and starts to pick up speed, the guideposts change and are further apart; graduations, first job after college, dating, and perhaps marriage and family. As the descent picks up speed into the forties, fifties, and beyond, time is measured in five- or ten-year increments and the clicks cannot even be discerned. Only looking backward does one realize how much of the track has passed and how far back it had been since they got in the car in the first place.

Reflecting on his life while sitting on his bench, it was unfathomable for Jonah to think it had been thirty years since that first meeting with Michelle's family. From that day forward, the coaster ride seemed as a beautiful blur while the car coasted closer to its terminus.

Their ride was not without bumps or jerks in the tracks. One such bump was significant, hurtful, and had the potential of interrupting Jonah's future ride with Michelle.

Parked in front of her apartment, the late summer air wafted through the open pickup windows carrying the scent of desert sage that grew in the foothills. They often sat in front of her apartment. Soon she would rent her own apartment, then roommates would not be present to inhibit their conversations and other after-date activities.

As was customary when Jonah parked his truck, Michelle slid over to the middle of the bench seat. She took control of the music on the radio/cassette player in the middle of the dashboard. Tonight, she was in a mood for soft rock, so she twirled the knob right away from Jonah's country station and rummaged through the stations, settling on one playing Amy Grant.

The couple talked for a while until their occasional nibbles morphed into continuous deep kissing.

After a few minutes, the couple separated. Both sat back against their seat and recovered while catching their breath.

Jonah had tried to define his feelings to himself for several weeks. Although in his mid-twenties, he had never felt the way he currently felt. He knew how he felt but saying it out loud seemed a gamble. His mouth was no longer wet from the kissing. It was now so dry and pasty that his first attempt at words crackled out until he cleared his throat. He began again.

"Today was fun. I don't get many chances to be around a family."

"You were great with the kids. It seemed natural."

"I found myself paying much more attention to you than anyone else."

"You perv," she said playfully.

"Well, that too, but I really enjoyed watching you when you didn't know it. The way you glided across a room with joy in your eyes, the way you interacted with everyone, how respectful you were to your parents, heck even the way you scratched your nose was endearing."

"Awe you're sweet."

"No, it's different than being sweet. I was smitten by you today. I've had growing feelings for you lately.

"And for the first time in my life, you are the one I'm going to say it to.

"I love you, Michelle."

After all his consternation, saying the words wasn't as hard as he thought it would be. It felt right. If felt comfortable.

He was surprised at her response. "I love you too, Jonah." It was so simple with no build-up or explanation. He supposed it was easy for her because she said it so often to friends and family. He was raised in a family that didn't verbally convey their sentiments very often.

Even though she didn't make it as much of an event as he had, he felt as though she meant the sentiment just as sincerely. At least, he hoped she did.

They continued seeing each other exclusively and settled into a rhythm that was comfortable for both. They were moving toward some goal, just neither one could define it.

She settled into her classroom at Neumann Elementary. At night, Michelle prepared her daily lessons at the kitchen table in her new townhouse, and during the day, she delivered the preparation. She was completely dedicated to her students. Jonah found her determination and passion very sexy.

One of her favorite quotes was the Latin, *Acta Non Verba—Deeds Not Words*. Jonah had this quote etched in a small stone that she kept on her desk at school. He was impressed that as competitive and talented as this beautiful soul was, she was humble. She never boasted of her own accomplishments, but let her actions speak for themselves.

Jonah accepted the position of manager at Mountain Impact when Andy was promoted to an area manager position. At twenty-four, he was the youngest store manager ever and the only African American manager in the company.

As summer forfeited to fall, the couple fell comfortably into their new routines.

Jonah flipped back the hood on his blue Nike windbreaker as he entered the store to become a hunter/gatherer of bachelor essentials. Still needing some ramen and Vienna sausages, he turned the cart around a corner and bumped into the cart of a woman about his age.

"Oh sorry," he said, quipping, "it's a good thing I've got insurance."

"No problem."

"Hey, do I know you?" the girl asked.

"I don't think so. I'm Jonah"

"Oh, that's it! We've never met, but I know Michelle. She showed me a picture of you once. Now, I know why I recognized you. I'm Beth"

"Nice to meet you, Beth."

They shook hands.

"You should come hang out with us sometime, Jonah. I'm surprised Michelle hasn't brought you around when we get together at my house. She said she would do it sometime but felt as though you would feel like the token black in the group."

Smiling insincerely, he asked, "did she actually say that? Token black?"

"Oh yeah, a couple of times. She was just joking of course."

Although the comment caught him off guard, he pressed forward with the conversation, and they parted promising to see each other soon.

The change of seasons along the Wasatch Front does not worry about the constraints outlined on the calendar. One year the chill can freeze the remaining flora and produce in early October catching most people by surprise. Trick or Treaters are frustrated to wear their perfect costumes under heavy coats. The very next year, superheroes and princesses run from house to house pursuing candy while wearing only t-shirts and shorts under their regalia. In those years, snow may not make its appearance until the turkey is done.

Whenever it arrives, winter is always much as this night was for Jonah. The wind pushed the sleet sideways as it started to change over to snow. When he left his apartment earlier that day, he dressed in khaki shorts and a hoodie. By evening, he longed for his parka and jeans.

With head down, he pushed against the wind to the respite of her covered porch. He rapped three times quickly in succession hoping the cadence would signal his urgency.

Expecting him, Michelle stepped quickly through the living room and pulled the door open.

"Oh, you poor thing. Get in here."

She removed his hoodie completely to reveal a dry Utah Jazz Karl Malone jersey underneath.

"Come on in, can I get you some coffee or hot chocolate. It won't take me long."

"I haven't had hot chocolate forever. Would you mind making me some?"

"I wouldn't have offered if I minded." She winked as she turned toward the kitchen.

Jonah followed her and straddled an oak barstool at the counter.

"How was your day, Hon?" He asked.

"Pretty stressful, actually. We found out about some new testing requirements the legislature is requiring schools to put in place. The union is fighting it for us, but we've got to assume we'll have to do it. It means changing our complete lesson plan to teach toward the tests. It's not right for the kids, but we'll see what happens."

"What about you? Did you enjoy your day off?"

"I just slept in a little, did some laundry, and went shopping for a few things."

"Sounds about right for a day off," she said as she finished off the hot chocolate. She had poured the powder into a mug and covered it with steaming water from the coffee maker. "Here ya go."

"Thanks." Jonah pulled the cup to his mouth but realizing it was a liquid inferno, set it down again instead.

Still looking at the mug steaming on the counter in front of him, his top two fingers linked through the handle, Jonah spoke.

"I've got to ask you something."

"Sure, what's up, Babe?"

"Today at the store, I ran into one of your friends, Beth. I'd never heard of her."

"Oh, Beth, yeah, she's one of my sorority sisters. I've known her since we were freshmen. A group of us still get together now and then. I'm glad you got to meet her. What did she say?"

"She recognized me from a picture you had shown them."

"Well, I've got to show off my man."

Michelle took her hot chocolate to Jonah's side of the bar and sat on the stool next to him.

"Michelle, she said you called me a token black!" He paused. "Did you actually say that?"

She stammered slightly while collecting her thoughts.

"Well, I guess I may have used those words, but it was only in fun while I was telling them how in love with you I am."

Turning his head to finally look at her, he said, "I can't believe you said that. It's so insulting. Why would you say that?"

"As I said, Jonah, it was just in fun. Maybe I'd had a few too many drinks."

"That doesn't make it better. In fact, it makes it worse, because the alcohol is allowing you to say how you really feel."

Jonah looked directly into her eyes. If not for the betrayal he was feeling, he would've seen her searching for the right thing to say recognizing her blunder.

He continued, "it's so unlike you, at least what I thought you were."

"Jonah, you know that's not me. You've never seen me do anything that even remotely says I'm prejudiced."

"Until now!"

"I don't even see color, Jonah."

For the first time, Jonah raised his voice. "That even makes it worse. I don't want you to not see my color. I AM MY COLOR AND MY COLOR IS ME! You can't separate it!

"I realize that I don't always act as the stereotypical black man. I listen to country music, I hike and fish and I'm not great at basketball, but those are all just that, stereotypes. I don't march in the street or take up African American causes, but I'm still part of that culture!

"My parents raised me to act mainly as a white man because I lived in a white man's world. Right or wrong, they thought that was the best road to my success in life.

"But I AM BLACK! My mom and dad were both raised in the fifties and sixties when they had fewer rights than whites. In Arkansas, my mom's family lived in a black ghetto where they were seen as second-rate citizens.

"Her dad was a sharecropper in eastern Arkansas where he got very little reward for all his backbreaking labor.

"I am the descendant of slaves who suffered unimaginable conditions for a hundred years before being freed.

"I am the descendant of some unnamed negro who was forced on a ship in Africa and sold in America!"

Jonah's voice had elevated with each point. He now reached an uncomfortable crescendo. Michelle was not concerned about her safety because he had never shown any propensity toward violence. She was just sad to have wounded him.

"I may not have always been true to my heritage, but I sure as hell won't let you take it away from me!

"It's not ok not to see my color!!"

Swiping his hoodie off the counter, he headed for the door.

"Stop, Jonah. Please stop. Let's talk about this."

He stopped at the door with his hand on the knob. Turning his head only, he said, "I have never had anyone who I felt the way I do about you. I thought you felt the same way. Now I'm wondering if I was only a sideshow to you, a novelty." He opened the door. The blowing snow shot past him into the living room.

"Don't leave, Jonah. I love you."

The door closed with a thump behind him. For the first time in their relationship, doubt hovered in the air.

Chapter 11

Angel Gabriel

The waves of heat rippled up from the concrete of I-15 near Bountiful, Utah. August in the desert rarely offered relief from the heat. Residents never counted on rain but headed to the mountains for the natural coolness it offered.

At least the air conditioning was working in the Sampson family van. Sadly, that was about all that was working. They had pulled off just a few miles north of Salt Lake City. Their 2002 Kia Sedona which had been overheating off and on for most of the trip from Montana, would not cool off. Steam poured out from under the hood, enveloped the car, and made it almost impossible for the driver to see enough to drive.

After driving on surface streets for six or seven blocks, the family pulled the steam wagon into a dealership that had a garage attached. The dealership was a substantial used car dealership with no brand affiliation.

The family consisted of young parents in their late twenties and two young boys, both under five years old. The holes in the older boy's jeans were obviously well earned as he played on the floor with his hand-sized dump truck. He made the noises of the truck, at least as he imagined them. The younger boy sat on his mother's lap holding a bear that was so worn from his affection, that it was doubtful the bear had been out of his hands during the three years of the boy's life. This boy lacked energy eventually lying his head on his mother's chest.

Even the older boy's playing turned to whining and finally to napping as the day wore on.

At the corner of the waiting room sat a man behind a magazine. The man's voyeurism of the young family was accomplished unnoticed above the top of his magazine. He couldn't help but think that the family's story was something that could further his purpose. While the mom tried to stay positive with the kids, the dad was very concerned about the repair and what it would mean for their travels. Dad sat bent over with his elbows on his knees and his hands forming a shield hiding his eyes.

The voyeur stood up unnoticed and quietly moved across thirty feet of carpet and tile to the service desk

"I know this is an odd question," the man said to the employee, "but do you know what the story is on the young family in the waiting room?".

Well, there's no such thing as mechanic-client privilege so the employee answered, "yeah, it's kinda sad. They were on their way from Montana to take one of their boys to Primary Children's Hospital." It was obvious to the stranger that the family's situation had been a shared discussion in the dealership that day. "I don't know what kind of condition he has, but I guess they were going to try some kind of new procedure on him.

"The dad works on the family farm, and they don't have much money. Their van overheated on the freeway, and they waited too long, and it looks as if it completely ruined the engine. We're working on it, but things don't look good. The mom and dad aren't sure what they are going to do. They don't know anyone around here. They'll probably have to get a rental car, but I'm honestly not sure if they can afford it. I guess they are planning on staying at the Ronald McDonald house for free while they are in town.

"By the way, we just finished up with your car, they're pulling it around right now."

The man thanked the employee, retrieved his car, and drove away.

After sitting in the waiting room for three hours, the service manager walked over to the stressed parents and sat down. The scene resembled those times in movies where a doctor approaches the loved ones in the waiting room to tell them their family member has passed.

The name stitched on the man's shirt was Marty. He said to the parents, "Well, it's as we suspected, the overheating was so intense, it caused some of the inner workings to seize up." He felt no need to go into the actual mechanical reasons.

"What's it going to cost and how long will it take?" The mom asked while reaching for her husband's hand.

"Well, it'll cost more to fix than the car is worth. You'll just have to junk the car."

The wife was clearly distressed. She was trying to search for a solution while holding back tears.

"As bad as that news is, I've got something to tell you that I think you are really going to be happy about. To tell the truth, I've never seen anything like it."

This got both parent's attention and they waited with new anticipation as he revealed the mystery.

"About an hour ago, a man walked in and spoke to the owner, Rob. The stranger looked around with Rob at some of the vehicles on the lot. After they negotiated a while, the man pulled out an envelope and gave it to the manager and told him it was to pay for the newer van on the lot that they had discussed. Here is the part that blows me away. He said it was for the young family in the waiting room with the two little boys. He said to complete the paperwork and title it in their...YOUR names!

"Now the Van is not new, but it's only a couple of years old and it cost him $20,000!

The dad stood slack-jawed, staring in disbelief. The mom was looking around quickly in disbelief, as happy tears ran down her cheeks.

"What? This can't be happening," The dad exclaimed. "I don't believe it!"

"Oh, it's all true," Marty assured.

"Where is this man? I've got to meet him. We can't accept such an offer." The wife protested as she looked around the dealership lobby.

"He's long gone. I'm pretty sure he wanted it that way."

An hour later—after all of the paperwork had been completed to ensure the new vehicle was in the family's name—they pulled out of the parking lot. Onboard were two extremely grateful parents and two very sleepy boys.

The memory of the event touched Rob, the owner. The philanthropic giver had made Rob promise to not tell of his identity. Rob actually didn't know his name, but obviously knew a description. The anonymity was a condition of the sale. Rob had not even considered looking at the man's service paperwork to retrieve his identity. The dealer hadn't promised not to tell the story generically, though. He felt as if others needed to hear of the event that happened in his showroom that day.

Rob knew a man at the Salt Lake Tribune. Rob's acquaintance was in sales and his dealings with Rob had been in advertising the dealership. Rob called his friend and was happy when he answered.

After some quick small talk, Rob told his friend the story of the giver. His friend was also touched by the story and said he would pass the information along to the proper reporter.

A few days later, Rob received a call at the dealership from Patrick Sobeno a Tribune reporter.

"Rob, Simon talked to me about the event that happened in your dealership last week" Patrick started.

"Incredible, isn't it?" Rob asked.

"It really is a great story," Patrick continued, "On its own, it would be a great story, but probably not newsworthy.

"About a month ago, I got another report similar to this. I just put it aside thinking it was nice, but not print-worthy. But coupled with this, it may be interesting."

"Oh really?" Rob exclaimed, "What happened?".

"There was this family out on the west side of the city. They consisted of a mother, father, and four boys, as I remember. The dad worked at the mine and the mom worked part-time at the school her kids attended. The oldest boy was graduating from Hunter High School. He was a smart kid and had accepted a full academic scholarship from Stanford.

Quite an accomplishment. Although all his fees were paid for, he still had the basic costs of living he had to be concerned with. The family had been scraping by for years to save money for their kids' college, expecting they would go."

Patrick paused his story for a moment and Rob could hear mumbling as if he had put his phone on his chest while talking to someone in the office.

"Sorry about that," Patrick continued, "Anyway, everything was looking great for the son, until the dad lost his job at the mine. The parents reviewed their financial situation and realized that the money that was set aside for college would need to be used for household expenses until he found another job. Stanford would have to be delayed."

"No one knows the background and how it all came to be, but one day when the mom was in line at the bank, a stranger walked up to her, and gave her an envelope saying, 'this should help your son still go to college'. She looked at the envelope, back up and the man was already almost to the door, so she didn't get to say anything. She stepped out of line and went to one of the standing tables where customers fill out deposit slips. She slowly opened the envelope. It contained $20,000 in cash! Sound familiar?"

"Whoa!" Rob exclaimed, "That's incredible".

The Tribune reporter continued, "I wanted to see if I could get a description of your guy and see if it matches the description of the other guy".

Rob replied, "Well, to be honest, I promised him I would keep his identity secret. I'll tell you a little about his appearance to help you verify, but I can't help much beyond that. He was a guy with darker skin, probably in his late 50's. Maybe 5'8", medium build. He had a goat-tee and a cowboy hat. That should give you enough to compare."

"Sounds like the same guy the mother described, although she didn't get as good of a look as you did. Keeping things anonymous, I want to run with this story. I'll just say, 'a car dealership in Davis County' if that's ok? I'm pretty sure the man wants it kept anonymous, so I want to honor that. It will be a good human interest story for the paper."

Rob jumped in, "It's hard to believe someone would be that generous to people he doesn't even know. I'd love to know his story. I wonder if he's done other things like this?"

Well, I guess we'll find out when I run the story. I'll let you know if I hear anything. Thanks for your time, Rob." The reporter hung up.

The story ran a couple of days later. As they say in the press, 'the story had legs!' Not only did it get the attention in the paper, but a couple of local TV stations jumped on it and ran the story. In the next week, Patrick received an additional five reports of the generous man who he had dubbed 'Gabriel' for his angelic generosity. In each case, Patrick kept the description to himself as verification of the validity. All the descriptions matched.

Over the next several months, Gabriel continued his anonymous giving and each time, the press would report it. He was able to keep his identity unknown. He started showing up with a hoodie instead of the cowboy hat apparently because, with his notoriety, he was afraid of getting outed.

◆ ◆ ◆

Before entering his office, Boley adjusted the rear-view mirror of his newest Audi to admire his recently styled slicked-back hair. Most people in the Salt Lake area were aware of Frederick Boley, Attorney at Law. One could not be oblivious to his omnipresence. Mr. Boley had become a local celebrity because of billboards, phone book covers, and bus benches that advertised his personal injury practice. He invited people in with catchphrases such as, "Fight 'em with Fred!" and "Fred is in your corner!" His ads featured pictures of him wearing boxing trunks in a ring leaning on the ropes.

Fred's law practice lured accident victims and other similarly wronged clients with promises of getting what they deserved—minus his forty percent contingency, of course. Fred's income had yet to find the ceiling. His ostentatious lifestyle was seen in everything he did; the cars he drove, the houses he owned, and the women he dated and occasionally married. His wardrobe consisted of flamboyant shirts with a top button or two undone—with sparse hairs peeking out—revealing much of his inordinately priced gold chain from Vegas. His teeth were brilliantly phosphorescent white, and his hair showed signs of unnatural attention. His unusual dark tan was a mix of Cabo San Lucas, tanning bed, and spray tan. Long ago, Fred had been Caucasian, but it appeared he was running away from it for a perceived sexier look in his late forties.

Because of how much he spent on local advertising, he expected to be treated as a king by media executives in town. On one occasion, one of the editors at the Salt Lake Tribune was buying him an expensive lunch—which Fred ate very little of as a power play.

"What can you tell me about this man 'Gabriel' that I don't already know?" Fred asked his dining partner, seeking inside information

"Nothing really," The editor said. "we've pretty much put everything we know out there already."

"Except who he is or how he looks," Fred excepted.

"We don't know who he is or even exactly what he looks like. We've kept the description under wraps for his anonymity. We know he doesn't want to be found out, so we protect that, but I'll tell you, Fred, you could even pass for Gabriel. We know he has dark skin and is about your age and build. The editor laughed, "Are you sure you're not the Angel?"

"You never know," Fred said with a wink.

Fred Boley planned his coming-out party over the weekend. On Monday morning he scheduled a meeting with Patrick Sobeno of the Tribune. He knew he would get an appointment because no one in the media would deny him.

At two on Monday afternoon, Patrick strolled into the law firm in Cottonwood Heights in the foothills on the way to four of Salt Lake City's immediately accessible ski resorts. Obviously, Fred had not only spent his money on his personal possessions but on adorning his office as something out of *Architectural Digest*. Patrick couldn't help but think Fred had nothing to do with the decorating and probably had paid six figures for a professional to adorn it in modernist extravagances. He wondered how the clients felt about parking their Dodges and Fords in his parking lot, then walking into this indulgence.

Patrick checked in with the receptionist who sat behind a teak desk worth more than her yearly salary. She looked as if she were someone who had followed Boley home from the tanning salon. All makeup and hair were in perfect condition.

Fred didn't emerge for another ten minutes, another passive-aggressive move he often used.

"Mr. Sobeno," Fred greeted, "I'm Fred Boley, nice to meet you." As if Patrick and the rest of Salt Lake City didn't already know. "Thank you for meeting with me, please step into my office."

The spider might as well have said, 'step into my parlor'. The office was as large as many houses of his clients. Once again, it was decorated with tasteful modernistic furnishings and artwork.

"Please, have a seat," the attorney directed.

"Thank you for taking time out of your busy schedule to come meet with me," Fred said, condescendingly.

"I'll get right to the point, Patrick. I've been wrestling with myself about whether to come out about this, but after a lot of soul searching, I think it is for the best. You see Mr. Sobeno," He paused to feign humility. He reached into the recesses of his mind to remember how that felt,

"I'm the man you call Gabriel"

Not surprisingly, this revelation caught Patrick completely off guard. He always imagined Gabriel to be someone who hid in the shadows waiting to lunge out into the light only to bless peoples' lives. Mr. Boley was the antithesis of that. Fred Boley spent his time being the spotlight.

Despite the reporter's surprise, it could certainly be possible. Boley undoubtedly had the means to do the giving. He did roughly fit the description from the eyewitnesses. Patrick had learned from covering the crime desk at the newspaper that eyewitnesses are notoriously unreliable.

Patrick finally spoke, "Wow! That's quite an announcement."

Not sure yet if he understood what was happening, Patrick started his questioning, "Why did you decide to reveal yourself?"

"Well, you see, I originally started doing it as a way to give back to the community that has been so good to me," Fred was finding it surprisingly easy to ride the humility wave. "After a while, I began to think, why should I keep it a secret? By coming out, I might inspire other successful people to use their money to bless the lives of their fellow man. Maybe I could start a trend of philanthropy throughout the city, maybe even further. Maybe it could even go viral, and the world could be affected."

This certainly seemed plausible to Patrick. Boley could still get his kudos by getting the story out while creating a philanthropy virus.

Patrick pulled out his digital recorder and began asking questions; the when, where, why, and how. Over the next hour, Fred answered questions vaguely about the events and precisely about himself.

Patrick had no reason not to believe Mr. Boley and was not doing an investigative interview, so he didn't ask the questions he should've. Although not what the reporter had envisioned about Gabriel, Fred certainly had means, motive, and opportunity to be the giver. The reporter composed the article, and it was published on Thursday. The same TV stations picked up the story and broadcast it on Friday. The mystery of Gabriel was solved.

Over the next few weeks, Fred refused interviews with any reporters or talk details even with his friends. His law practice got huge PR press and his client list started growing as never before. His philanthropy had done more for his business than all the billboards and bus benches ever had. The people who knew him had a hard time reconciling his actions.

Jonah had read the reports of Gabriel and now was intrigued with the revelation that he was actually a very wealthy local businessman. He was surprised that the same personal injury lawyer that he had always thought of as a weasel who took advantage of people in their time of devastation had a good heart after all. To be honest, he had a hard time believing it. One thing he had learned from his days on his bench was that people aren't always what they appear to be to the world. People often spend their life hiding their whole being. Frequently, individuals don't want the

world to know their inner demons or, apparently, their angels.

Randy Judd

Chapter 12

The Cowboy

Two weeks after Fred Boley came out of the closet revealing his philanthropy, Jonah had an interesting conversation with a Fide.

After finishing up with a young mother who just needed to vent about her struggles with being so overwhelmed, a man approached the bench and sat down. The man's cowboy hat was worn from decades of use at his ranch. Tilting it to the front, he scratched his head through his thick, dark hair. His worn jeans were frayed around the small holes that had worn through during riding, roping, planting, and praying. Scuffed leather on his brown cowboy boots conveyed that these were his work boots. On a more formal occasion, his boots would probably be completely shined to a gloss, bejeweled or other adornments. His skin was brown but lighter than many Hispanics. The man's age couldn't be readily determined. The leathered skin from sun, dust, and work made him look much older than his five decades would've if he had sat behind a desk.

After Jonah introduced himself to the vaquero, he went through his spiel about the rules; confidentiality, nothing illegal, and no counseling. It came time for the stranger to reveal his inner thoughts.

His introductory stammering allowed him to catch his thoughts. "I come to Liberty Park sometimes when I'm in town."

Most people would ask where he was from, but Jonah learned that many people did not want him to know more than they were willing to divulge.

"I saw your flyer down by the pavilion. The more I thought about it, I thought you might be the perfect person to tell. Do you guarantee this is confidential?"

"As long as it's not something illegal that I shouldn't know in the first place,"

"Oh no, nothing like that. I just need to make sure it doesn't go further than this bench, you understand?"

Jonah nodded reassuringly.

"I'm a rancher by trade. I don't like people much, so I rarely come into town. When I do, it's just for a few hours to get supplies. I come here to the park because I enjoy the greenery. My ranch is out in the desert so not a lot of trees and grass. It's nice here.

Over the years, I've been very successful. My parents brought me here from Mexico when I was just five. We were so poor that we often slept in our pickup truck. My father got a job as a ranch hand out past Grantsville. I watched and learned and eventually became a ranch hand also. Long story short, As I grew into an adult, I eventually was able to get a small ranch of my own and things just grew from there. Most people wouldn't guess that I'm a very wealthy man now. Especially by the standards of where I came from.

"Well, my parents are both gone, I have no brothers or sisters. I never got married. I was always too shy around women. Of course, I have no kids."

Jonah's usual posture when listening was turned slightly sideways with his left knee resting on the bench. This position allowed him to look at the Fide without staring directly at them. He felt as if this made them feel less threatened when they were revealing their secrets. He always encouraged them to continue talking with a nod or saying something as simple as 'Ok' or 'Go On'. That is how he sat today, listening to this old cowboy.

To the cowboy, eye contact was uncomfortable. He sat leaning forward with his elbows on his knees as he told his story, looking directly at Jonah when he felt something demanded more seriousness.

He continued his story, "With so much wealth and no one to share it with, I started to feel that I was quite selfish. All I've been blessed with, and it's all just sitting in properties, my ranch, and cattle.

"A couple of years ago, I started to give large amounts to charity. I still do, but I wasn't finding as much satisfaction as I thought I might. I guess because these charities are so large, I couldn't feel I was helping individuals.

"Then, one day a year or so ago, I was in a supermarket here in town and I was behind a young mother who had a couple of rowdy kids she was trying to manhandle. You could tell by her clothes that she didn't have a lot of money to support her little family. When she went to pay for her groceries, her card was declined. Embarrassed, she told the cashier she wouldn't be able to take the groceries that had already been bagged and were waiting for her. I know most people would've done this, but when I offered – insisted—on paying her bill, I felt a new kind of fulfillment. It wasn't because of her gratitude or because it made me look good. As a matter of fact, the attention from the woman, cashier, and bagger kind of embarrassed me. I felt good because I had made a difference in her life.

"As I left the store that day, I started thinking about how I could make a difference. I wasn't going to just sit by the register all day and buy people's groceries, but I could do better to be aware of people's needs around me.

"First, I started noticing other places where I could help financially. If someone was doing a fundraiser for their school, I started giving more than just a twenty-dollar bill, now hundred-dollar bills. If someone was along the road with a flat, I would take the time to help them and if they needed a new tire or tow, I would pay for it.

"I started to look at stories in the paper of people I thought I could help. Every trip to Salt Lake or wherever I needed to go for business, I would look for a way to give. It was important to me to be anonymous. Otherwise, I felt as though I was doing it for the accolades. I certainly wasn't, I just wanted to help. I've got an amazing amount of self-worth knowing I'm sharing with others who have not been as fortunate in life as I have."

Jonah turned to him, and their eyes met. He saw a genuine man. One who had a great soul. He hadn't made the connection yet—though most people probably would've.

He paused and then spoke again, "I'm the man they call Gabriel."

The conclusion that Jonah should've made was made for him.

"But the man who is Gabriel has already come out," Jonah said.

He addressed the objection, "I know. When I read it in the paper, I couldn't believe it. Even though I hadn't wanted any attention for the gifts, I certainly didn't want some fraud lawyer to get credit. I don't like lawyers much anyway."

"If this is true," Jonah interjected, "Why are you telling me and why now?"

"I've been stewing over it during the last two weeks. I don't have anyone that I could tell, but when I saw your flyer, it was a quick decision. I'm not sure what I do now."

Generally, when a Fide was through with their story, he would find a way to end it, ask if there was anything else or even if they felt better for telling their secret. This time, Jonah couldn't let it go.

"If you *are* Gabriel and Fred Boley isn't, what now? Do you want me to tell other people or call the newspaper or…what? Why would I even do that, just on your word?"

"No! I still don't want anyone to know. I want to stay anonymous," He answered.

Jonah looked within himself for ideas. Although his first inclination was to think the man was making it all up, why would a good, honest man such as this be interested in taking credit for something as magnanimous as what had been done secretly to individuals?

Jonah finally broke the silence, "If Fred Boley isn't really Gabriel, what if there was a way I could expose him without revealing you?"

"How would you do that?" he questioned.

"I don't know, let me think about it," Jonah paused. "How long are you in town?"

"I leave in the morning."

"Is there any chance you could come back in the morning before you leave? I would ask you for your phone number, but I know you want to stay anonymous, and frankly, I don't want people to have my number either. Could you do that? It would give me a chance to think about a way that we could make this work."

He thought for a second, "Yeah, I could do that. I didn't come here to make a big deal about it. I just wanted to get it off my chest."

"Yeah, I know. I just want some time to see if I have any ideas to help you. I may not, but I want to give it a try."

The cowboy stiffly got up from the bench and walked over to shake Jonah's hand. "And it's all confidential, right?"

"That's right."

He turned and shuffled away. The years of riding, roping, and ranching had turned the once virile farmhand into a stiff, aching shadow of what he had been. What he could no longer do physically, he could now make up for financially. Jonah's mind was pondering on how to proceed. With no other Fide on the waiting bench, his mind was reeling for a creative solution. First, he needed information to verify the stranger. To do this, he needed to find out things that were not readily available in the newspaper. He needed to talk to the Tribune reporter.

A few minutes later, Jonah stepped away from his bench into the shade of a tall pine tree. Dry needles cracked under the rubber soles of his Reeboks as he asked the receptionist to put him through to Patrick Sobeno. The receptionist connected him immediately. He speculated Mr. Sobeno wasn't significant enough to have his calls screened.

After the reporter's initial greeting, the caller started, "My name is Jonah Freeman. I was talking to a man today at Liberty Park that told me some interesting things about an article you wrote about Gabriel."

"Oh really?" he half-heartedly responded as if distracted by something else on his desk. "Has he got another story about Lawyer Boley?"

"Actually, just the opposite. He essentially says he is the real Gabriel."

Patrick was intrigued, "Go on."

"He seems legitimate. He's a rancher and apparently has a lot of money. He doesn't have any family to leave it to and wants to give a lot of it away to help people."

"Why would he tell you? What's he to you?"

"Well, it's a little hard to explain. I go to Liberty Park a few days a week and people come by to talk to me, not just socially, but they tell me things that they don't feel as though they can tell anyone else. This man heard about me and came to sit on the bench and tell his secret."

"Hmm, That's strange. I want to talk about your story later. For now, what's this man's name?" Sobeno said, reaching for a pen and paper.

"What I do when I listen to them is provide anonymity. I never …seldom know their identity. Mr. Sobeno, I'm a pretty good judge of character and I feel he is genuine."

There was a moment of silence as Patrick got his thoughts together. "Let's just say he is. That would be a huge story. *Big time lawyer takes credit for philanthropy he didn't perform!* But obviously, I can't move forward on something some cowboy told a man on a bench in the park."

Jonah responded immediately, "Oh, I understand completely. I thought as the writer of the story, you probably knew some details that hadn't been in your stories. Something I could test him with."

"That's an interesting idea. I couldn't just tell you. You'd have to ask him some questions that I give you and you provide me with his answers. Give me some time and I'll get back to you."

"I'm meeting with him again in the morning. Can you get back to me this afternoon?" Jonah requested.

"Sure. I just need to reach out to a few of my contacts and get some details."

That afternoon, Patrick Sobeno called back. He gave Jonah four questions that the public wouldn't know.

First, with the young family that had their car break down, what was the make and color of the vehicle that was bought for them?

Second, with the mom and boy who were approached at the bank and given money, which bank was it, and who else was with the mom and son?

Number three, when the money was dropped on the porch of the family whose dad had just been diagnosed with MS and could no longer work, what was the money in?

Fourth, the family that had their house broken into on Christmas Eve and all their presents stolen, on what street did they live? That was kept from the story for their protection.

Jonah thanked him and told him he would call him back tomorrow, assuming the man showed.

◆ ◆ ◆

The freshly woken sun glistened off of the dew of the morning grass. The dawn moisture isn't common in the desert city of Salt Lake. Activity at the park was a little subdued as the coolness of the morning discouraged some of the usual crowd.

The Cowboy appeared stealthily from somewhere behind Jonah. The stranger not wanting to be revealed, parked on the other side of the park away from the bench.

"Hey, Jonah. Did you think of anything?" Jonah had told him his name the previous day. His identity didn't need to stay anonymous.

"Actually, yes, I've got some ideas, but first I need to ask a few questions that will help validate your story. I went to the reporter who wrote the story and got some details the public wouldn't know."

"You promised me that you wouldn't tell anyone about me," he said raising his voice.

Jonah put up his hands as if he was showing he was unarmed. "No, I didn't tell him anything but the basics. You've got to understand, if I'm going to put my neck out, I've got to know you're legit."

"I don't know if I want to do this," he protested.

"Look," Jonah continued, "if you are indeed who you say you are, we want to use the information to dispute Fred Boley for taking the credit. If you aren't who you say you are, you'll owe me an apology for thinking badly of Mr. Boley, even if I already think he's a weasel."

"Ok," Cowboy relented.

Jonah looked down at his list. He didn't know how much detail to accept but decided he would determine that as they proceeded.

"I'll ask these questions assuming you are who you say you are."

"First, when you bought the young couple the car up in Bountiful. You do remember that, right?" He nodded. "What was the make, model, and color of the car?"

Not sure how this interrogation was going to work, the cowboy waited until he was sure the question was complete to respond. "It wasn't a car. It was a Dodge Minivan, a Caravan. I don't actually remember the color. It was either Light Blue or Gray. How'd I do?"

Writing down his answers, Jonah responded, "I don't know the answers, I'm just going to report back to the reporter."

"Next, when you went to the bank and gave the mother and her son some money for college what bank was it, and was there anyone else with them?"

"It was one of the big chains. Chase, no wait, U.S. Bank. It was just off of Bangerter Highway in West Valley. Let's see, who was with them? Let me think. Of course, the mother and son. It seems as if there was another one. Another child, but I can't think. Oh, wait! It was a boy because I thought he reminded me of one of my ranch hand's sons."

It took me a minute to get all the details down. I didn't want to miss anything that would sway the decision one way or another.

"Ok, you dropped off a lot of money on the porch of a family whose dad had just been diagnosed with muscular dystrophy. What was the money in?"

He replied quickly with no thought, "I put it in a pizza box right in front of the door, knocked, and ran around the corner until I knew they had it. Also, the dad had multiple scleroses, not muscular dystrophy."

Jonah had slipped in that lie on purpose. Impressive!

"The last one is this: The family who had their house broken into on Christmas Eve and had all their presents stolen, what street did they live on?"

He thought for a minute. Jonah wondered if he had stumped him on this one. Rubbing his chin as if in thought, he finally spoke slowly, "Normally, that would be a tough question. I don't remember directions or addresses easily but in this case it's easy. They lived on State Street, right across from the soccer stadium in Sandy."

He had answered all the questions so confidently, Jonah did not doubt that he was authentic. There was no way that a man such as this would spend the time necessary to know these things. That is, unless he is lying on the fly, and he won't be seen again.

As they parted, Cowboy said, "I will be in town on the fifteenth to get equipment to take back, will you be here?"

"I'll make sure I am. That will give me time to validate you and put a plan in action for you to review."

The cowboy's brow was crestfallen by the term 'validate', but he let it pass.

As the cowboy walked bowlegged in his boots across the park, Jonah thought there was a fifty-fifty chance he would ever see him again.

When he called Patrick again, the reporter didn't answer. He left a message. It was pretty obvious that he was anxious to hear from Jonah because he called him back soon after Jonah had stuffed the phone back into its home in his jeans front pocket.

When he read the answers back, Patrick didn't verify them individually but said that was an amazing amount of detail. He asked if Jonah could come into his office to discuss the stranger, but the Listener could see people lining up to talk to him, so he made the Fides his priority.

"If you can come to the park, and introduce yourself between other people, I will make time for you."

He seemed completely confused at the operation.

A little while later, Patrick stepped up to introduce himself at an opportune time. Jonah was having a natural break between Fides. He offered a place on his bench and the reporter sat down.

Patrick Sobeno was a much younger man than Jonah had envisioned, late twenties or early thirties. Jonah had to look up to the man to greet him. As Patrick looked down at Jonah, his fashionable styled hair fell in front of his eyes. In a somewhat predictable look for a reporter, he had round metal-rimmed glasses.

"Let's talk about our situation, here Jonah," he started. "To be honest with you, I'm not sure what to do. If this man is truly Gabriel, then Fred Boley is a huge fraud. I was asking myself on the way over here, why would he do it? The only answer, if it is indeed true, is for notoriety for acts that were meant to be anonymous. If that's the case, then it's not only immoral, but probably criminal, but let's not get ahead of ourselves, we've got to make sure your man is the real deal. When can I meet him?"

Jonah responded rather matter-of-factly, "well, you can't. He was very clear that he wanted to keep his anonymity. He didn't tell me his name and he even parked his truck somewhere else so I wouldn't see what he drove or his license plate. I'm supposed to meet with him on the fifteenth when he comes back in town, but there is no guarantee he'll be back."

"What did he look like, anything resembling Boley?" The reporter asked.

"Well, I haven't paid that much attention to Boley," I answered, "but from what I remember, he could. He's probably older than the lawyer, but the build is about the same from what I remember. The biggest difference is Boley is white, and the cowboy was Hispanic, although not very dark."

"Actually," Patrick interrupted, "Boley spends so much time in the tanning bed, he's probably darker than most Hispanics."

Both men paused for a moment. Patrick became very aware of the beautiful day. The morning dew had long since said adieu and the sunshine pushed aside all clouds and established its dominance for the rest of the day. Patrick couldn't help but be jealous of the environment that Jonah could call his office, while his own office was cramped, dark, and sitting in the back of a noisy newsroom.

Sobeno continued, "so, if this is true, then Boley is a snake and as rotten of a person as I've ever seen. I need to do some more investigating behind the scenes before I make any moves publicly. Something interesting happened when I called the car dealership up in Bountiful. The owner, who had been full of details the first time I spoke to him, was very cold to me this time and gave me just a few details. I started thinking, I wonder if Boley got to him. I did a little research and found that Boley had previously filed an injury lawsuit, but after Boley came out, the suit was dropped. I think there must be a story there too."

Jonah spoke, "I thought a lot last night about how we could take care of Boley. At first, I thought an article by you would embarrass him and almost certainly hurt his business. That sudden slowdown in business could hurt other attorneys and employees at the company. Then I started thinking, what if we got creative with him and negotiated something that would not kill his business and his hundred employees, but would both punish him and do good at the same time?"

Patrick was intrigued, "what did you have in mind?"

"I'm not really sure yet, but maybe some way that we don't reveal him if he doesn't take any more credit for actions and promises to privately fund more benevolent actions."

"Hmm, you may have something there. Let me think about it too. In the meantime, I will do some more digging, verifying and asking a few more questions than I did in the first place."

Patrick changed the subject, "So tell me, Jonah, what's this all about?" He said as he looked around and slightly waived his arm."

"It's a park. That's a lake." Jonah replied smugly.

"I mean what are you all about? You told me on the phone that people come to you to talk. Did I hear that right?"

Jonah reached in his backpack and gave him one of the flyers, the kind he had put up near the restrooms in the park.

"Basically, I'm a listener. People come to me to tell me secrets; sometimes sordid, other times funny, but always something they didn't feel they could tell anyone else."

Patrick wanted to complete the thought, "and you give them advice?"

"Actually, no. These people don't generally want advice. They just want to clear their heads, and often their conscience of something they've been carrying with them for a long time. Sometimes decades. If they ask me what I think, I'll occasionally give them my thoughts, but only occasionally. I have no training to counsel them."

"I've never heard of anything like this. How did you get started?" The reporter was naturally inquisitive.

Jonah spent the next ten minutes or so telling him about his background in business. He gave Patrick an overview—especially about his marriage to Michelle—and how he had accidentally tripped on this listening idea which had become one of the most rewarding things he had ever done.

The reporter seemed intrigued.

Jonah looked to the benches where people waited to confide in him. There were two ladies there. He excused himself and Patrick shook his hand and left, promising to call him before the fifteenth. The reporter walked to the edge of the tree-lined park and glanced back at the listener already engaged in the first lady who needed to cleanse her soul.

The two men talked several times over the next two weeks. They worked out the particulars of their plans. There were many moving parts that all had to come together flawlessly.

On the fifteenth, Jonah arrived at his office in the park a little earlier than usual. Occasionally, someone would be on his bench when he arrived. He couldn't take a chance on missing the man who he and Patrick referred to simply as *Cowboy*. Tossing a coin would've been as accurate as the chances he felt of Cowboy appearing. The brief rain an hour before his arrival, brushed the grass and trees jade green. After securing his bench, he welcomed his first Fide at nine o'clock. After the visitor had talked to him for about twenty minutes, telling him the woes of his childhood dog that he had never gotten over and his wife wouldn't let him get another, Jonah saw Cowboy sitting on another bench about fifty feet away. Jonah compassionately handed the man a box of Kleenex which he always kept close. Unlike his usual benevolence, he guided the session to an early end so he could summon Cowboy over.

"I'm glad you came back," was his simple greeting.

"I almost didn't, but my curiosity got the best of me, to see what you had come up with," he replied taking his seat on the bench.

Cowboy's jeans were not frayed as much this time. Instead of his cowboy hat, he donned a green John Deere baseball cap.

"I think we've come up with a great plan to share with you."

"Who's 'we'? You said you would keep this confidential. You gave me your word!"

Justifying himself, he promptly replied, "I got the reporter involved more and we've come up with a plan that I wanted to run by you. If you don't approve, we won't do it, but if we don't do something, I guarantee that Boley will continue to take credit for your generosity. Nothing in this plan will reveal your identity."

Cowboy seemed cautiously interested, "what's the plan?"

Jonah laid out the framework of the plan because they had not worked out the specifics yet.

Their strategy was outlined. They would approach Boley with the revelation. He would deny it. They would give him proof, maybe a test similar to what they had given Cowboy. He would threaten them in some way. They would provide him with an alternative to being exposed which would also benefit the community.

Cowboy seemed amiable, "but I will never be exposed, right?"

"That's correct. Remember, I don't even know your name, what you drive, or where you live. There is one thing that has to happen, though."

"What's that?"

"You've got to meet the reporter. He is not willing to risk his reputation or maybe even his job on my word alone."

Gabriel sat pensively for a few moments. He then replied, "ok. I guess you've gotta do it that way."

"Great! He knows I'm meeting with you, and he is waiting for my call to come over." Actually, Patrick was in his car at the edge of the park watching the bench from afar and waiting for the call. He waited for a few minutes after Jonah texted him to make it look less as though he was lurking.

As he approached, Patrick was introduced to Cowboy. The reporter asked the man some very general questions to verify some things that hadn't been covered with the questionnaire a few weeks before.

"I want to thank you, sir," Patrick told the man. "Your generosity is so unbelievable. You've done these things out of the goodness of your heart with no ulterior motive. I can't imagine how many of the world's issues would be resolved if more people acted like you."

Cowboy bowed his head in both modesty and embarrassment, "this is exactly why I don't want anyone to know but thank you."

Patrick was touched by the man's humility, "I give you my word sir. I will not reveal your wonderful secret, but you can hold your head high knowing the good you've done. You're a good, good man."

They both shook hands with Cowboy and said goodbye. As he left, both turned subtly and looked away as he crossed the park to his pickup honoring his anonymity.

Neither Jonah nor Patrick ever heard from this giant of a man again. His presence continued to namelessly bless strangers in town.

The two had devised a meticulous strategy and were anxious to put it into action

Randy Judd

Chapter 13

Overcoming Obstacles

The phone rested on the avocado laminate kitchen counter of the apartment. Jonah and two of his roommates shared a common phone. The fourth paid more for the master suite which came with its own phone line. The outgoing message on the common phone was generic. Originally, the roommates, all in their early twenties, had tried to be clever with the recordings. Eventually, they realized how stupid they sounded and chose one that would help them sound more mature.

When Michelle tried to contact Jonah over the next few days, all she could do was leave a message. She couldn't plead too much on the recorder knowing the roommates would all hear it.

Jonah listened to all the messages, sometimes two or three times. Her sweet voice on the phone implied pain although the average person wouldn't have been able to detect it. She disguised her aching heart well for the others who would be listening. Jonah didn't return any of the calls. He wasn't able to define his feelings yet.

Had he overreacted? He didn't think so. The person you love shouldn't be so flippant about something so important. Still, was it enough to end a relationship that was going so well? He loved her still. If they could get past this bump somehow, he felt as though he could forgive her. It would take a change of heart on her part.

During the same time, Michelle was distraught. The night he stormed out, she prostrated herself on her bed and cried for the next hour. After gaining some composure, she called her mom who was always a great confidant and shared great wisdom.

After getting the recap, her mom was unapologetic in her response to her daughter. "I don't know how, but you've got to make this work. I see the way you two interact and how close you've gotten. After we had him over for dinner, I watched your love blossom. It's worth fighting for."

"But mom, what if he doesn't want anything to do with me after what I said?"

"We all make mistakes, and your mistake was extremely hurtful. All you can do is find a way to beg him to forgive you. You'll have to let him know that you'll never do anything like that again and he's got to believe it."

She left messages but knew constantly calling would look needy on her part and she wanted to show she was strong.

On Friday night, as Jonah approached his truck after work, he was reminded of the stormy night because slush and muck still clung to the side of his vehicle. He intended to get it washed so it would be sparkly even for a few days before the next storm. Maybe tomorrow he would.

The streetlight in the parking lot gleamed directly down on his truck creating an angelic halo around the mucky vehicle in the darkness. As he approached, he spotted a paper under the wiper. Assuming it was a sales flyer that had been put on all cars in the lot that day, he tiptoed and stretched to retrieve it. The paper was overprotected by a plastic bag. That seemed a lot of trouble for an advertiser.

Standing in the empty parking lot with the halo of light above it and a clear star-filled sky beyond that, he opened the plastic bag. Inside was an envelope with his name written in cursive and heart drawn where the envelope had been sealed in the back.

The night air was crisp, but wind was absent, so instead of entering his truck, he leaned against the fender. The only thing that pierced the quiet was the popping of a semi's airbrakes several miles away in the canyon. He slowly pulled the flap open and retrieved the letter.

This was a message he couldn't ignore as he had those on his answering machine. Unlike the messages on the machine in his apartment, Michelle could expose her feelings to Jonah without the sentiments being shared with others.

My Dear, Dear Jonah,

My heart aches as I think about the way things ended on Monday. I've tried and tried to reach out to you. Now it's apparent to me that you don't want to hear from me. I simply cannot let this go without letting you know of the heart-wrenching feelings I'm having.

I was so wrong to have done that to you. No amount of apologizing is enough to convey my complete disgust in myself for what I said.

Your words were so passionate, and they let me know how deeply you were hurt. To know that I wounded you so badly and so profoundly is tearing me apart.

Please, please forgive me!! Please talk to me so that we can work this out. My heart is torn, and I cannot stand to be without you. I not only want you, but I NEED you!

I will love you always,

Michelle

He read the letter twice, the second time gently touching the words with his index finger. In his mind, he could hear her delightful voice narrating the words. In the still night air, a breath of perfume rose from the letter.

Over the last few days, Jonah had explored his thoughts and emotions regarding Michelle. Convinced he hadn't been wrong in his proclamation to her, he wondered if he could've done it without hurting her. No, it needed to be said. She needed to understand those things if they were going to move forward. He explored his own relationship with his culture of which he was now even more proud than he had been before that night.

From the street, the only light emitting from the townhouse was from her second-floor bedroom. Standing at her front door, he hesitated. Jonah had never been comfortable with conflict but didn't assume there would be any tonight. He could hear her footsteps coming down the stairs after he rang the doorbell. Watching the peephole, he saw the light disappear signaling she was looking out. After realizing who it was, she opened the door slowly.

Michelle's eyes were red and swollen, her cheeks were flush. She leaned against the door frame and sheepishly greeted him.

"Hello, Jonah."

"Hi Michelle, I got your letter. Do you think we could talk?"

"Yes, I need to."

Dressed in only a tank top and short shorts, she led the way. Jonah was pleased to follow. They took seats on opposite ends of an overstuffed couch in her living room. Each had the leg hoisted up on the couch making it easier to see each other.

"What did you think of my letter??

"Thank you for taking the trouble to bring it out and keeping it safe in the bag." Jonah showed an impish grin which softened the tension a tad.

"I've been such a wreck since Monday. I took days off work because I couldn't function. The only time I've left the house is to bring the letter to you."

Jonah had noticed how unkempt she appeared.

"I'm sorry I didn't take your calls. I've been struggling with the whole thing too. I've been doing a lot of introspection: finding out who I am, what I think, and what my values are. Aside from the heartache, which has been horrible, this week has been good for my growth as a man."

Michelle absorbed all he was saying still not sure where all of this would lead.

"So where do you stand?" she asked.

"As I thought about it, the things you said felt to me as though you hadn't quite accepted all of me. You still put me in different categories instead of simply Jonah." He looked down at his interlocking fingers resting in his lap. Not that he cared about his hands, but it was somewhere to focus while he thought.

"An individual's description is always defined by different categories: Race: Black, White, Asian, Mixed. Hair color: black, blond, red, bald. Size: tall, short, fat, slim. Personality traits: Friendly, happy, sad, motivated, OCD, mean, amiable, so many personality traits. At the end of the day, though, we are all unique. The only way to describe me is to say I am Jonah. My mix of emotions and the way I see the world are totally unique. There is no one else like me. I am Jonah Freeman, the one and only. Until you can know Jonah Freeman inside and out, you won't really know me. That's what I need you to do. See me as an individual, not categorize me with everyone else."

"Oh, Jonah. That's what I want. More than anything. I think I've got a good start, but I want to do everything I can to learn who Jonah Freeman is and to love everything that you are."

"And I want to learn everything about Michelle Bohnan. I love everything I've seen so far and I'm sure I'll love everything there is to know."

"I'm sure you'll agree we'll never come to a place where we know everything."

"I absolutely agree but when we get to a place where we know we enjoy what we've found so far, we should be able to accept anything else that comes along. I know this is a bold statement, but at this moment, I think I want to spend the rest of my life getting to know you. Is that something you want to work toward?"

"Jonah, you have taught me to love as I wasn't sure I could. I have seen how great my parent's life is together and wanted that for myself. I wasn't sure if I ever could, but you've made me feel that maybe I could after all. Let's continue to work on it and at some point, we'll feel it's right."

With this, Michelle went to Jonah with arms open and then attacked his face with a flurry of kisses eventually settling on his mouth. Both said, 'I love you' with deeper affection than they had ever felt before. The next morning as the dust danced off the sunrise light beaming through the window, the couple felt their future was bright also.

The next summer, Michelle and Jonah exchanged vows in an outdoor ceremony at Alta Ski Resort. The wedding was light on pomp and circumstance but still attended by many friends and family who wanted to share the joy with them. The mountains towered above with their approval. The green slopes rose until they encountered last winter's snow still clinging on to the higher peaks.

The beauty of those snowcapped mountains surrendered and bowed to Michelle that day. As she emerged with her father from a nearby building, the attendees were completely mesmerized. Wearing her floor-length gown which she and her mother had lovingly created, the bride-to-be had a hypnotic effect on the gathering. As she walked between the parted folding chairs, Jonah could not take his eyes off her. She insisted on wearing a pair of new hiking boots hidden underneath. Her best friend Veronica stood by the altar as her maid of honor and her youngest sister proceeded as the flower girl.

Jonah's family was all able to attend. Isaac and Joseph stood near Veronica at the alter and served as Jonah's best men.

The day couldn't have been better for the bride and groom. The celebration continued into the night, and they were both ecstatic to be joined permanently.

Her family was disappointed that they hadn't married in her family's church, but since she hadn't attended in several years and they believed in agency, they supported the couple in their decision. Jonah was endeared to Michelle's family and was truly happy to call them his family also.

Jonah and Michelle Freeman built a house in Millcreek on a quarter-acre lot. The new house was styled as a charming rambler with three bedrooms and two baths, very typical for the new subdivision. Not knowing how their future family would look, they also built an unfinished basement in which they could expand. Their house was a basic starter home. Their salaries combined didn't qualify for much more, but that was ok with the couple. They both prided themselves on being simple people and they loved bumping against each other as they tried to pass in the hall, the kitchen, and especially the bedroom. Looking like a scene from Norman Rockwell, she often worked at the kitchen table while he finished dishes fifteen feet away.

The first spring, they planted a little garden and cared for it occasionally. After a few seasons, they gave up their green thumb project. They loved that house and everything they shared there. The young couple hadn't planned on it, but the little house on Snowcrest Lane became their home for the rest of their lives.

A few years came and went in their home in Millcreek. As much as they cherished the house, there was always a siren call from the mountains, both winter and summer, but unlike in Odysseus' case, answering this call gave them contentment. To them, the time together was sacred, and the granite slopes of the mountains were a perfect place to worship.

Socially, the two outgoing personalities attracted many diverse friends. Although they often hosted many friends, they were happiest when they were together alone. That's the way it should be, but many couples use their acquaintances as an escape *from* their spouse.

Once the couple had become one, they felt the desire to become three. They both wanted children, so the discussion wasn't hard. Having grown up in a large family, she imagined them having several kids. He was sure about the idea of kids, but not quite on board with having a houseful. Jonah too had such great memories of his own family. He was close to his brothers and could see the happiness they were having in their own young families.

One night after an extended shift, he sluffed up the front steps and sluggishly walked through the front door. No matter what type of day he had, he could always count on Michelle's presence to enlighten his mood. Not that she ever met him at the door with his slippers and the paper, but just her existence made him happy. On this night, his sweetheart was on the couch. It was the same overstuffed couch she had brought from her townhouse. Sitting in the familiar groove she had created over the years, she sunk until the cushions enveloped her. She almost always greeted him sweetly, but on this night, there was a special excitement as she asked him to sit beside her. She thought about all the clever ways to tell him, but in the end, simply smiled and said, "I thought you would want to know,"—she hesitated for dramatic effect—"we're going to be parents!!"

To say he was elated would understate his emotions. Not even asking her to repeat herself, because he knew he heard it clearly the first time, he took her face between his hands and kissed her so firmly their lips popped as they released. She shared the details. She had just taken the test that day and would go soon to see a doctor. Her announcement wasn't a total surprise, since they had been trying for a few months. Understanding she was successful in everything she did, it wasn't surprising that she was able to get pregnant so easily. They knew that it wasn't this easy for everyone, having friends who were not so fortunate.

The time of anticipating their first child was magical. Aside from Michelle's serious morning sickness, they spent much of their time waiting and getting prepared for their child. The description is trite, but her countenance did glow. Michelle was thrilled to be a mom and talked often about how their family time in the mountains would look. She described it in detail. She assumed their child would ski by the time it was three years old. Jonah pictured her bringing the newborn home in an Eddie Bauer backpack.

A man of many pet peeves, Jonah cringed when people said that THEY were pregnant. While it was true that THEY were going to be parents, Michelle was the only one in a state of pregnancy. While he would help as much as he could, she would be doing the majority of the hard work during the next nine months.

The Freemans spent time creating a nursery in a bedroom in their house which had previously been occupied by various exercise and skiing equipment. Being able to determine the gender of a baby was new and they were excited to find out to know how to decorate.

About six weeks after Michelle's maternal announcement, Jonah got a call at work from the principal of her school. Michelle had started bleeding and had to be taken to the hospital by ambulance.

For Jonah, the ten-minute trek to the hospital was a blur. He drove through several stop signs and lights slowing only slightly to watch for oncoming cross traffic. During the race to the hospital, he worried about what could be wrong. He had no experience in gestation and only had a rudimentary knowledge of exactly what was happening within her body to grow their baby.

The emergency room nurse pointed him to the room where his wife was being held. When he got to the room and threw back the curtain, he was frustrated to see no bed and no Michelle. A nurse who had seen him go in asked who he was, then told him they would have Michelle back in a few minutes. The nurse wouldn't tell him anything else except that she was not in any danger.

Every minute in the alternate universe they call an emergency room seems like thirty in the outside world. He finally saw her bed being wheeled into the room. He immediately went to the head of her bed. Her eyes were closed, but she was not asleep. Slowly she opened her teary eyes.

Jonah leaned over while reaching for her hand through the chrome bars of the hospital bed. Inches from her face, he spoke softly, "Sweetheart, are you ok? What's going on?"

Through her crying which wasn't uncontrollable sobbing but a heartbreaking whimper, he heard the crippling words. "I lost the baby, Jonah. I lost the baby."

Jonah was devastated and joined her in the cacophony of weeping. Jonah had never been an overly expressive person when he was emotional, but he still felt strongly just the same. At this instant, he couldn't hold back the tears and the crying made him convulse.

Seeing Michelle, he knew her grief must be unimaginable. He pulled her to him, and they continued to mourn as one.

After the initial shock, their sobbing eventually subsided. He continued to hold her head against his chest as she lay in the bed. Jonah wanted to ask all the questions of how, why, and when, but did it really matter? Their child was never to be.

The attending obstetrician came in. Doctor Mary Richards was typically dressed in her white lab coat and stethoscope resting on her neck. In her fifties, she had no doubt delivered this kind of news many times over the years. To her, it must've been routine, but she had to realize that anytime she did, it was devastating. The tests performed when Michelle was brought in made Dr. Richards think something was wrong with Michelle's uterus preventing her from carrying to full term. Dr. Richards was concerned that Michelle might never be able to carry a baby but needed to do more tests. In a few days, they got the dreadful news that they would never be able to have children, at least not naturally.

The school year was about over, so Michelle took the rest of the quarter off giving her the whole summer to convalesce physically and emotionally.

During the next few months, they navigated new territory and later remembered this part as the toughest of their marriage.

In the nineties, depression and its associated treatments were just emerging in the mainstream. Neither Jonah, nor any of his family, had been burdened with mental issues so he didn't know how to respond when her doctor diagnosed Michelle with depression and started her on treatment. The doctor said what she was feeling after the loss of the baby was not so different from postpartum depression.

Jonah was at a loss as to what to do for his lovely wife. His simple mind assumed depression was something she could just snap out of if she only had the right positive atmosphere. He treated her as if it were some type of character trait rather than an actual illness. Surely, if she just exercised, watched lighthearted movies, ate healthier, meditated, and so on, she could cure herself.

Sitting on his bench in Liberty Park so many years later, he realized how much of an ass he had been. If he had treated her with the same concern as if she had cancer or a heart attack, he would've been better support for her. His low point was when he took her by the shoulders and firmly shook her and told her to snap out of it. His feelings of shame for that incident remained with him.

Generally, it's in men's nature to fix things. If they can't fix problems, they don't often have a second approach. Jonah recognized his shortfall, after so many years.

Veronica was Michelle's best friend over the years. They taught at the same school and the same grade during the start of their careers. Jonah called her Verny. She was single and spent a lot of time at their house as a surrogate part of the family. During Michelle's depression, Verny wore angel wings in aiding Michelle, being there when she needed her, and staying away when she didn't.

Jonah eventually learned that the best he could do was to be there for her, hold her when she needed him, and not try to be her psychiatrist. She didn't need him to try to fix her. She needed his unconditional love. He learned all of this too slowly over her struggle.

Looking back, they had been fortunate. Michelle's depression was situational and slowly got better with counseling and medication. They had friends who dealt with the condition all their lives. Jonah and Michelle felt genuine compassion for their friends' struggles. Jonah did not doubt that going through this alongside his sweet wife had helped him on the Listening Bench.

As summer recess started to come to an end, Michelle was able to feel hope. Hope didn't happen overnight, but by her first day of class, she had improved enough to put on a fake smile and confront her new fourth graders. Fortunately, the smile didn't remain fake for too long. Michelle was back.

The couple didn't talk much about the loss of hope of having children. They discussed adoption, but for whatever reason, didn't pursue it. They accepted the sad reality and moved forward. They knew for the sake of their marriage, they needed to adapt. They could not get over it but had to move forward despite it.

As the coaster continued along the track, they both progressed in their careers. Jonah was promoted to district manager and eventually moved into a position within the home office. He found his work rewarding. He was fortunate to have advanced as far as he had without a college degree. He never felt completely fulfilled, as if this current place in life was his purpose, but he was very grateful for the station in life he held.

Michelle was able to emulate her dad's path in education. She became the Vice Principal at her Elementary School, then after several years, was promoted to Principal at Whitley Elementary in West Jordan.

Michelle was fortunate to have several great friends. Some for many years. Her best friend over the years continued to be Veronica. Through the years, they developed such a great friendship that they were practically sisters.

Veronica never married. She attended the Freemans' events periodically with companions. She even had a few serious relationships, but the associations never developed romantically enough to last long-term. Verny settled into the life of a forever single, but she felt good about her situation and made a great life for herself. Along with her teaching career, she had a circle of close friends and family, so she felt fulfilled.

Michelle and Jonah continued to cherish their time with each other in the outdoors. They stayed very active, but as their ages progressed, the activities were necessarily less strenuous. When Jonah was in his late forties, much of his activity became limited. One day in late February, the couple was skiing at Brighton Ski Resort. The winter storm which was forecast came to fruition facilitating whooshing down the hill in knee-deep powder. Stupidly, they were going too fast for the low visibility caused by the blowing snow. Sprinting into white darkness, they had no surety of what lie beyond. Jonah was about fifty feet ahead of Michelle. Not knowing the run as well as he thought, he came upon a group of trees too quickly to react. He plowed through the smaller evergreens and slammed directly into a large one. Michelle saw his demise as she approached and was able to avoid the trees and stopped quickly to help him.

Jonah had shattered his leg; broken in several places. The recovery and physical therapy were long. He was never able to do strenuous athletic activities again, which explained to some extent his current dad's body. He made sure he did everything he could to make certain that Michelle still got her fill of activities, but the outdoor activities that brought them together in the first place, would have to bow to other endeavors.

It was at this time that Jonah and Michelle began going to Liberty Park several times per week so she could still stay active, and he could do as much as he and Wilhelm were capable.

Randy Judd

Chapter 14

Their Final Chapters

Marriages can never be perfect because, simply, people can never be perfect.

The more a couple tries to convince others that their wedlock is flawless, the more one suspects it isn't. Jonah's dad had told him to always be leery of a man who touted his honesty. Abel told him that was the time to put his hand over his own wallet. The same could be said with those touting a perfect marriage.

Matrimony doesn't have to be perfect to be deemed successful, though. Resembling the waves at the seashore—which appear on the sandy beach then recede into the abyss—any marriage is volatile at some point.

Some marriages appear as successful business endeavors; each partner has their assigned duties and responsibilities. Together, they make the business run efficiently. Without establishing emotional intimacy, the couple finds themselves in trouble when the kids leave and each other is all that remains. Then, they either must reinvent their relationship or live their years in loneliness while their partner is as close as the other end of the couch.

Sometimes to avoid this, the parents do everything they can to prevent their children from leaving home. As with all animals, the ultimate goal of a parent is to prepare the offspring to survive on its own and leave the security of mom and dad. That is the whole purpose of parenting.

Jonah certainly didn't know anything about raising kids and steered away from advising on the subject. A friend once told him, 'I did my best parenting before I had kids.' So maybe Jonah could still advise, but he didn't.

Jonah and Michelle's marriage wasn't perfect. They each had issues that the other saw as troubling. Michelle was a lot of great things, but tidiness was not one of them. Coming home each day, Jonah had to take a deep breath before opening the door from the garage. He never knew what landmines of clothing— washed and unwashed —, sporting equipment, dishes still in front of the television, or magazine and books he would have to delicately step over. He had learned over the years that it was just easier for him to pick up and organize rather than grumble and fight about it.

Jonah's trait that caused Michelle consternation was his tendency to impulsively spend their money. He never put their finances in jeopardy, but there were many things around the house that he had bought on a whim and had never used. They approached finance from different vantage points. Michelle believed finances were best used as security and Jonah felt it was foolish not to enjoy them whenever they could. Many marriages cannot survive a difference in basic financial outlook, but after arguing about these differences early in their marriage with little common ground, they chose to focus on each other's many good qualities instead.

As Jonah and Michelle's marriage passed the quarter-century mark, their relationship continued to evolve and mature. He thought her smile lines were well earned and she thought his salt and pepper curls looked distinguished. They had always been great friends. He preferred to be with her over anyone else he knew. She felt security in his arms and comfort by his side. As they aged, they spent hours on their back deck gazing at the mountains as they talked about everything, anything... and nothing.

Their union evolved to a point that they were more than just friends, lovers, and confidants. As trite as it sounds, they existed as one entity. They didn't take their relationship for granted. Many of their friends had found a happy relationship yet didn't experience the closeness of Jonah and Michelle.

The couple had reached a level in their careers where they had the discretionary income to do what they wanted. Having lived in the same house in Millcreek all their married life, the mortgage had been paid off. They started traveling as often as they could get away wanting to get as much out of life as they could before their bodies got too old to enjoy everything the world had to offer.

They traveled internationally. In Europe, they traced Michelle's family lines to the highlands of Scotland. They trekked to Edinburgh and drove three hours to discover her family's roots.

On another jaunt, they spent two weeks in Asia. The couple walked along the Great Wall, experienced the villages of Vietnam, the temples in Kyoto, Japan and the most vertical city they could imagine, Hong Kong.

They spent weeks exploring the United States and felt as though they would never be able to see all they wanted to experience.

Their happiest place was exploring their home state. With five National Parks and even more National Monuments, one could never see everything the Beehive State had to offer. They were still adventurers in their fifties, but because of their age and his former injury, the difficulty of the experiences had to be throttled.

In the summer of his fifty-fourth birthday, Jonah was summoned to a Friday afternoon meeting in the boardroom of his corporate offices. Also in the room were the founders and all the vice presidents and directors of the company.

Those in attendance were told that *Mountain Impact Sporting Goods, Inc.* was going to be sold to a national chain. Apparently, the discussions had been going on for a year or so, but those attending were still surprised. Jonah thought that maybe they shouldn't have been shocked. The founders were now in their eighties and none of their children seemed interested in continuing the legacy.

Of course, the biggest question for all in the room was what would happen to the employees and the family of loyal workers that they had nurtured and loved.

All store-level employees at the twenty-six stores would remain in place. The new company certainly needed them to continue to run the operations. That was a relief.

Unfortunately, the Salt Lake City office would no longer exist, and all corporate operations would take place in the acquiring company's headquarters in Dallas. All executives and upper-level management were to be let go. The founders did provide a severance package and most of them who were tenured had stock options that they would exercise.

As Jonah discussed the news with Michelle that evening, they were both a little disoriented. They had no debt and with the severance, stock options, and 401k, they knew finances wouldn't be an issue. After all, she still had her principal position at the school. The apprehension was really what would become of Jonah. He was too young to retire, yet too old to start something new.

His career had mostly been one of happenstance and circumstance. As a child, no one says they want to be an executive at a large sporting goods store when they grow up. As with most adults, Jonah had gotten where he was through a series of choices that had consequences that led to where he was today.

Jonah had never felt really fulfilled as a person in his career. He sometimes would find volunteer work in the community to fill some of the voids. One day while setting up a company bar-b-que at Murray City Park, he noticed a homeless man shuffling by before the event. Instinctively, Jonah waived him over and loaded a plate of food for him, gave him a bottled water, and sent him on his way. Later that evening, he saw the man approaching their pavilion again. Jonah wondered if he was coming back to get more food. To his surprise, he handed Jonah a bag of caramel popcorn he had gotten—may have stolen—from a convenience store. This event caused Jonah to think, that if he just walked through the park handing out bottled water to the indigent, he would probably get more satisfaction than a month's work in his office. Was there something resembling that out there for him?

Michelle totally supported Jonah in finding a sole-fulfilling purpose in his life and following whatever calling he could. He started looking for possible solutions, but in the end, he believed that calling would have to find him and not the other way around. He just needed to put himself in the right place for inspiration. He was feeling very joyful, anticipating what lay ahead.

Waking up each morning semi-retired gave Jonah a whole new outlook on the world. No longer did he have to be at the office by a certain time. Actually, no one expected him…anywhere. That also meant he woke up every morning and said to himself, 'what today?'. At first, the new liberation was quite fascinating, but it only took a few weeks for him to realize that he needed a regimen even in his leisure. He planned his week each Sunday night, even as detailed as the daily relaxation activities. He wasn't too hard on himself if he strayed from the schedule, though.

He was able to do things spontaneously as never before. He visited Michelle at her school more than he ever had before. She delicately let him know that he probably should not visit as often. "Everybody loves you," she said, "but you may be becoming a distraction."

He seduced her into letting him attend the mid-fall assembly by telling her he would take her out to dinner afterward. She succumbed. Sadly, he didn't get to sit by her on the stand.

After almost two hours—which became increasingly arduous as time went on—, the program ended. Jonah helped clean up and they each drove their cars to their favorite Indian restaurant. Recently, they had developed a new taste for Indian food. Jonah had an employee from New Delhi who one day brought into the office an array of Indian food from her brother's restaurant. As luck would have it, Michelle was visiting him that day, and they both decided this was their time to experiment when they wouldn't have otherwise. Immediately, they savored the explosion of delightful blends of spices. A taste of their favorite dish felt as though the flavors were having a party in their mouths. They sampled a variety of dishes often during the next several months and then settled on their favorites: Butter Chicken for Jonah and

Coconut Korma for Michelle. The next step in their Indian culinary adventure was to discover the best restaurant for these delightful dishes. The winner was *Saffron Flavors of Delhi* in an older part of town near the University.

After meeting in the parking lot, they were greeted at the door by Sandeep, the owner. He greeted them kindly, calling them by name, and led them through the all-encompassing fragrances to a table. Too loud sitar music quickly faded into the background as their attention turned to each other.

As a couple and friends, they never had to think about what they would talk about. Their topics meandered in such a way that they rarely finished one topic before moving unawares to another.

After savoring the zest of the meal, they sank back into the vinyl booth to unwind and let the food settle. Eventually, they felt obligated to surrender their table to another couple waiting near the door. After dispensing a toothpick, he held the door open for her and they stepped into the soft rain of the evening. If he had an umbrella, he would've offered the chivalrous action and held it above her head, but he knew she wasn't delicate. He had seen her rock climb in a thunderstorm. The gentle rain painted the reflection of the streetlight onto the black canvas of the pavement as occasional vehicles swished past unseen.

As the couple arrived at his car, he spread his coat open for her, she entered his cocoon and they kissed. Her hair gave up its excess wetness causing the rain to roll down her cheeks slowly before continuing on its way. The cool rain did not deter Michelle from looking straight into Jonah's dark eyes inches away.

Holding his damp face between her feminine palms, she said almost in a whisper, "You know you mean the world to me, right? A lot of times I find myself wondering how I got so lucky. How we got so lucky. You are everything to me and I can't imagine life without you. I don't think it would be worth living." She nestled her head on his shoulder.

Suddenly, the rain intensified. The rain came down on them as an army of eager droplets sounding as applause hitting the ground. Jonah's response would have to wait. Shouting 'I love you', they both escaped to the shelter of their separate cars.

Jonah watched her drive off as the thumping of his windshield wipers indicated the intensity of the rain outside.

Before they parted, he let her know he had to stop for gas so she wouldn't worry as she often did. Inside the convenience store, he talked for a moment to one of his recent employees who he ran into. They trotted back to their cars in the rain and went their separate ways.

A half-mile before turning into their neighborhood, multiple blue lights strobed at the wet intersection ahead. Over the years there had been several accidents at this intersection, some serious. Jonah always hoped they wouldn't involve someone he knew, but tonight his hope was useless.

The first vehicle he saw was a large pickup truck with its grill area smashed. As he passed the policeman who was directing cars, the other car came into view. When wondering if the accident involved anyone he knew, he hadn't even considered the worst. Pushed up against a lamp post with its driver's door crashed in, was his lovely wife's Subaru.

In that moment nothing else existed. Jonah wasn't aware of anything beyond, only the impending tragedy before him.

He steered his truck to a quick stop off the side of the road before running to her car. His feet felt as though they were hindered by weights as he tried to get to her as fast as he could. She wasn't in it. Oblivious to the carnage of the vehicle or the blood inside, he turned to find an officer to ask about her. The cop interrupted his notetaking to tell Jonah she had been taken by ambulance to St. Mark's Hospital.

Having been trained to prepare for emergency situations in the mountains, Jonah thought logically before emotionally. He sped toward the hospital's emergency room and arrived in ten minutes. Knowing how tough Michelle was, he didn't entertain that she was hurt any worse than a broken arm or slight concussion.

The truck decelerated abruptly having barely stopped before he leaped out. He left his truck in the no-parking zone in front of the emergency room doors. After entering the lobby, he moved briskly towards the reception desk. He was told to sit in the waiting room until someone came for him. The waiting area in this emergency room was dismal, filled with both those patients who were triaged to wait and those waiting to hear news about their loved ones. There was a sad cacophony of moans, coughs, and crying. Jonah didn't look at anyone else fearing he'd see something he didn't want to engage with. The television in the corner added to the depressing atmosphere of the room by playing some twenty-four-hour news channel. As the adrenaline began to subside,

Jonah finally relinquished to the severity of the situation. He sat slumped, hungering for news, looking up with every opening door. The harshness of the accident replayed in his mind. The crumpled door behind which she had been driving was mangled and the impact that caused it was horrendous. Fortunately, the first responders had gotten there quickly and extricated her immediately.

Restless, he continually asked for updates. No one would give him anything except that Michelle was being examined. He felt very alone amongst the rows of seats. He called Michelle's parents. They were immediately on their way.

Forty minutes took forever for Jonah, but finally, a doctor came out and called his name.

"Mr. Freeman?" he asked, "you are Michelle Freeman's husband, right?"

Jonah replied, "yes, yes. She's my wife. What's going on? I prefer you be completely frank with me, doctor. I don't want to have to read between the lines."

"Your wife's accident caused major internal injuries. We are mostly concerned about her pancreas, but honestly, we can't say what kind of injuries she has until the MRI results are reviewed. I've got a surgeon on his way down to evaluate the results as soon as they come in."

Jonah was distraught of course, but his time in the wilderness had taught him the importance of keeping a level head during times of distress.

"Can I see her? I must go be with her!"

"She's sedated, but you can certainly go sit beside her. You may be asked to leave once the results are back and we review them."

Jonah didn't rush back, knowing she was sedated and not waiting for him to come dashing through the door, but he certainly got into the room quickly.

After shyly pushing through the door and pulling back the curtain, he cringed at what he saw. Amongst a tangled mess of cables and IVs and with the sound of beeping and assisted breathing, he was appalled and saddened by what he witnessed. Her face was bruised and bloody. One eye was swollen. Even as awful as she looked, through all the blood, bruising, and bandages, Jonah still recognized his sweetheart and best friend. He was overwhelmed with the love he felt for her during these moments. Not sure where it would be ok, he kissed very gently on her forehead and told his unconscious wife he loved her. Pulling a chair over beside the bed, he held her hand even though he knew she wasn't aware. He lightly rubbed each finger individually as he talked softly to her. This was so much more difficult than the last time she was in the hospital with the miscarriage. During that event, she was awake and aware, and they were able to work through things together, but this time he felt alone. With no medical personnel in the room, he couldn't hold back his troubled tears. Laying his head against her, he wept. His tears dripped onto her face. Not one to readily show emotions, there was no doubt about the pain he was feeling for her. In those moments, he did something he was not accustomed to doing, he prayed. He wasn't sure what to say to God or how to phrase his words, he just pleaded, both aloud and in his heart and mind. Pleaded for her not to be taken. Pleaded for her to be made whole.

Eventually, the doctors came in and Jonah was asked to return to the waiting room.

He was comforted to see Michelle's parents in the waiting room. They all moved quickly toward each other and embraced amongst sobs. Jonah brought them up to speed on all the details. Not that it mattered at this moment, but Jonah let them know that Michelle had actually run the stop light and the other driver was not at fault. Jonah had caught a glimpse of the other driver who seemed unscathed except for some face abrasions from the airbag exploding into his face. Jonah thought about the moments before the crash. Had she known she ran the light? Did she see the truck coming? Did she lose consciousness immediately or had she suffered? Jonah held Michelle's mom and they both cried. Her dad put his arm around his wife.

Within an hour of waiting, Jonah saw the same doctor enter the waiting room and walked directly toward him. Jonah stood up and took a step toward the doctor. Following his request to be direct, the doctor spoke, "I'm sorry Jonah, she didn't make it. She never woke up."

He thought his distress couldn't get worse, but it did. The three of them went to the room together to be with her. He warned Michelle's mom and dad what to expect, but it didn't prevent her mom from gasping when she saw her sweet daughter's condition. The medical staff compassionately gave the three some time with her. Her body was still warm when Jonah hugged her and cried and cried. His constant companion, his buddy, his lover, his sweetheart, his wife…was gone and he knew he would never be the same. Of all the things he loved about Michelle, his favorite thing was how much he loved her and that she was the type of woman who could evoke that feeling.

The funeral was held the following week. The temperamental October weather was producing sunshine. A beautiful day if you weren't watching the love of your life being laid to rest.

Jonah had lost people close to him before, but there was no comparison to the pain he felt in the coming days, weeks, and months. He thought the feelings he had could best be described as a yearning that couldn't be fulfilled. He felt the pain deep in his stomach and up into his chest. The bruise was not just emotional. he could feel it. Months later, when he told this story, he still felt the hurt.

A few weeks after her burial, the headstone was placed. The substantial piece of granite had an engraving of two coyotes: one black, one white. This was an homage to the animal she pointed out early in their relationship. Both of their names were on the single stone. Although there was no date below Jonah's name, the pain in him wished there had been. Above her name, he had requested the stone to be engraved with '*Acta Non Verba, Acts not Words.*'

Sitting on his bench almost a year later, he still thought of her almost hourly whenever his memory was sparked by something in the park…or nothing at all.

Randy Judd

Chapter 15

Comeuppance

T he day after bidding adieu to Cowboy, Jonah and Patrick met at the Tribune to prepare the plan. The men got as many of the predictable details worked out, but there were many volatile events they would have to decide on the fly since they couldn't precisely predict the lawyer's responses. Jonah agreed to go with Patrick to meet with Boley. Patrick felt as though his being there would add some validity to their claim.

Jonah asked Marvin—Fide number one—to attend to the bench while he was visiting with Boley. Marvin had been helping out on the bench lately either by helping organize the waiting bench or on occasion actually becoming the listener. Marvin listened compassionately to the people who came to share secrets. His gentle ways allowed people to open up even more honestly than they initially intended. Just as Jonah had, Marvin found purpose in being present to hear individuals who needed to share. He felt it made him a better man.

While in the Tribune office, Patrick called Boley's law firm to schedule an appointment. Jonah envisioned the teak desked receptionist asking with her whitened smile about the purpose of the meeting. Mr. Boley was out of town, she said, and she would have to check with him. Patrick gave a vague reason to make Boley wonder. The lawyer must've been intrigued. Maybe he thought the newspaper wanted to give him some type of accolade because the receptionist returned the call and set an appointment for early the following week after his return from his beach house in Cabo.

Now that the plan was in place, Jonah had mixed feelings. It would be wonderful to give Boley the reward he deserved, but he also was unsure of Boley's reaction and generally didn't seek conflict. Patrick, on the other hand, thrived during a confrontation.

The Listening Bench

On Tuesday morning, Jonah sat at a cushioned booth across from Patrick at the IHOP a few blocks from the law firm. Over his Rooty Tooty Fresh and Fruity, Patrick finalized the plan. Jonah's tension caused him to fumble with his utensils while undoing his napkin-enclosed bundle.

Boley had a strong personality since childhood, but it had gotten even stronger in law school and had increased since. He was purposely intimidating. Since he couldn't rely on his physical stature to be daunting, he depended on his skills at bullying and belittling his opponents through voice volume, facial expressions, gestures, and body language. Even the strongest opponents often came away disparaged resembling a cowering dog.

Jonah and Patrick knew their plan was a swing for the fences but felt they had the balls, bats, and karma on their side.

Upon their arrival, Patrick introduced themselves to the receptionist. They were then instructed to have a seat on the leather couches of the waiting area. Of course, Boley made them wait as a passive-aggressive show of power. He was currently just watching videos on Instagram.

After twenty minutes, they weren't led to his office, but to a small board room where Fred Boley met them with his imitation smile.

"Good morning Mr. Sobeno! It's good to see you again." Boley feigned sincerity. "And who is this with you?"

"Jonah Freeman." Jonah said, holding his hand out for a shake.

Pretending to not notice his hand, the lawyer looked back to the reporter for an answer.

"Jonah is a friend of mine who has some interesting information that I needed to review with you. I brought him with me today for additional support."

Boley, motioned for them to have a seat at the table as if he were one of the models on The Price is Right. Jonah and Patrick were on one side; Boley was on the other side facing the wall-sized window overlooking gardens and water features.

Sitting there in the man's lair, Jonah felt nervous, as a little boy in the principal's office. Patrick on the other hand looked amazingly calm and ready to pounce. Patrick realized Boley had used him as a pawn in his betrayal and that didn't sit well with the reporter. Although he was a much younger man, Patrick was ready to take control.

"Fred," Patrick said using Boley's first name to establish who was going to be in charge, "we know you are not Gabriel!"

Boley's countenance slowly changed from feigned amiability to impending rage. His forehead furrowed, his pupils dilated, the veins in his neck began to thicken, and his face undoubtedly turned red under his tan.

"How dare you come in here with such an accusation. After all I've done for the community, you have the balls to sit here and accuse me of lying to everyone?"

"Yes," was all Patrick said. He really does have cojones, Jonah thought.

Boley then turned condescending. "What information do YOU have to make such an allegation?"

"The real Gabriel," Patrick said smugly.

"Oh, is it this Jonah guy who walked in and tells you he's Gabriel and you take his word for it? He's not even the right race!"

Jonah thought it was time he stepped in to support his friend. "Oh, I'm not Gabriel, but I know who is."

Boley stared incredulously at him as if to ask, 'what permission do you have to speak?'. Boley's look at Jonah empowered him to speak. "I know the truth, and you know the truth. So why don't you save us some time and just stop pretending so we can talk about the next steps!"

The lawyer wasn't ready to concede. He rose from his chair as a boxer rises from the mat after a knockdown. He hoped it would improve his chance at intimidation during the rest of the match.

"I don't need to prove anything to you two. I'm Fred Boley, the most powerful attorney in Utah! I don't need to prove anything to you two peons. Do you know how rich I am? Do you know what influence my money can buy?"

Patrick responded to Boley's last statement but ignored the rest of his rantings. Patrick said, "Mr. Boley, I don't believe a man's character is determined by the size of his bank account! And in this case, that's certainly true.

"We are here to help you save face. If you want, I can give you the same test that we gave the real Gabriel. He passed with an A plus. What grade would you get…Fred?"

In an effort to skirt the question and accusation, the lawyer went on the offensive. "Don't you know I pretty much own everyone down at your paper?! When I call, they answer! When I want a five-star dinner, they buy! If I want a lowly beat reporter fired, they will do it in a minute!!"

Patrick quickly replied, "and if you did that, I would have no reason to not reveal what I know which would embarrass you and strike a humiliating blow to your company. You'd be run out of town! We're giving you a chance to get out of this without the truth being revealed.

"Why don't you stop all the chest-thumping, admit that we know the truth, and let's move on from here?

Jonah was impressed with how much gravitas Patrick spoke. This young man who earned just a small percentage of what Boley billed annually was in control and wasn't backing down. It was a marvel to witness.

Boley was still fuming but had stopped speaking. From his still standing position, he turned and walked over to the window. Staring out, he was obviously ignoring the stunning mountains in the distance and even the luxurious water feature immediately in front of him.

After a minute which seemed an hour, he spoke, "How much do you want? What's your shakedown going to be?"

Goliath had relinquished. David had beaten him, and it was spectacular to watch. All three men realized that there wasn't much need in arguing the truth.

Patrick had been reacting quickly to every insult and quip the lawyer had thrown at him. Now he paused. He let the significant moment sink in for everyone's sake.

Patrick and Jonah knew that with every minute of pause, Boley's perceived dollar amount was growing. The suspense was rewarding for the two men. The tension hung in the air as moisture over a humid Florida swamp.

Now that Patrick knew he had the putty in his hand, he started to mold it.

"We don't want your money—at least not for us. We've developed a plan which will allow you to save face, although we personally think you don't deserve any consideration. We feel that exposing you would hurt your company and although we despise you, we don't want to hurt the hundreds of people who work for you. We also feel all the good that has

come from Gabriel doesn't need to be tarnished by your cowardly acts."
Patrick was now taking advantage of the turn of events to take his own
jabs at the all-powerful lawyer.

Chastened, Boley returned to the table. Even in his worst loss in the
courtroom, he never felt as humiliated as he did now in front of these
two peasants. He knew his next words would show he had surrendered
to their allegations, but he had to do it anyway. "What's the deal?"

Patrick and Jonah wanted to jump up, chest bump, and high-five, but
they restrained themselves. There would be time for that later.

"Our demands are not complicated," Patrick began, "they are as
follows." He then pulled out their printed sheet of conditions and started
to read.

"First, you will not take credit for any more good deeds that Gabriel
does. If you want to continue to do charitable acts on your own, you
must give credit to your company or the employees of your company
but not to yourself personally.

"Second, you will not take any more interviews or in any way refer to
those acts of kindness that have happened in the past.

"Third, a charitable foundation will be set up by Jonah and me to give to worthy recipients throughout the area. You will anonymously donate $100,000 yearly to this non-profit LLC. We will actively solicit other donations in the business community, but you won't take any credit for your donations."

Boley spoke up, "I obviously know the law well enough to know this is blackmail."

Patrick acknowledged the lawyer's point, by looking at him, then continued anyway.

"The last point is that we will not tell anyone that you are not Gabriel. We won't tell our employers, our friends, or even our spouses. As of now, there are only four people who know the truth. If you choose to go to anyone to bring up our discussion, if we ever hear of this oral agreement outside of this room, I will go full-bore outing you with the truth. I will tell every news agency, every publisher, and every reporter I know. It will make a wonderful story that everyone in media would love to tell."

Boley, defeatedly asked, "What about this real guy? Won't he tell?"

Jonah felt the need to jump in. "We've sworn him to secrecy also." They hadn't, but he knew he could if they ever saw him again and the lie seemed sufficient for Boley.

The fabulous plan was laid out and Gabriel Boley was dethroned. They had given this scoundrel a way out. A way to avoid the humiliation he deserved and at the same time, provide a way of doing ongoing good in the community.

Boley, not being able to get out of his lawyer mode, said, "I'll have my assistant type up a contract outlining these things."

Patrick rebuked him strongly. "I laid out the plan less than a minute ago and you already don't get it! There can be no contract typed up by your assistant because YOU CAN'T TELL ANYONE!! There is no need for a contract, it is simple if you tell, we tell."

"By the way, if you record conversations in this room, you'd be smart to erase that recording as soon as we leave. This coming out will hurt you much more than it will hurt us."

With Patrick's lead, they both stood up. They didn't shake the disgusting man's hand to avoid the need for sanitizer afterward.

They held their celebration until they were out of his office and out of the parking lot. Jonah pulled over into the parking lot of a strip mall. When he looked over at Patrick. The reporter was smiling but shaking.

"I held it together in there, but now it's all coming out. For the first time in my life, I stood up to a bully and won!"

"You were spectacular, my friend! I really can't believe we pulled it off. What do we do now?"

"Nothing, for now, we'll need to watch everything he does for a while and see if he takes us seriously. I'll start forming the nonprofit and, in a month or so, we'll reach out to him for his first installment. That will be the sure sign that he took it seriously."

They stopped at a bar for a quick drink. Jonah took the rest of the day off. Since it was a Tuesday, no one was expecting Jonah at the park. He took Wilhelm into the mountains. The dog bounded out of the car and into the trees. Jonah followed slowly.

His thoughts turned to Michelle. The corners of his mouth turned up slightly and his lips parted to reveal a slight smile when thinking of her, but his eyes still moistened. The man longed for her companionship.

A few nights later, Patrick and Jonah met for a celebratory dinner at a local family-owned Chinese restaurant. Patrick knew the owner by name, and they were given a table in a private area where the owner had many extra items brought to them on the house.

The men talked about their new non-profit organization and a little about how it would function. They settled on the placeholder name of Angelforward, LLC.

After reveling in their victory over Boley, Patrick turned the discussion to another topic. "Jonah, I want to write a story about you."

"Why would anyone be interested in me. My life story is nothing special."

"I'm sure your story is amazing, but that's not what I'm talking about. I want to write about this extraordinary gig you've got going on down at the park."

"Why would I want you to do that?"

"Two things, really. First, it is very much the kind of story I do; feel good, human interest. Second, I think it could help you be a benefit to even more people. Let me ask you this. Would you want more people to come to talk to you? Could you handle more?"

"Yes, I don't think I've even tapped the need. I've also got Pam and Marvin who have helped on occasion. Honestly, they are just as good as me."

"If I did a story, I bet we could find all kinds of people who would want to talk to someone. We could maybe reach so many that Marvin and Pam would get all the chances they want to help."

Jonah unknowingly rubbed his chin as he thought about the possibility. After seeing so many people with so many things to tell, he knew he wasn't reaching even a very small portion of them.

After biting his bottom lip slightly, he agreed. "Let's do it!"

Patrick placed a digital recorder between them. Doing this allowed him to focus on Jonah and not on writing notes. They talked for an hour about how the process started, what type of people came to the bench, and how many people he talks to in a week. Patrick asked for some examples of the stories. Jonah gave generalizations but wouldn't divulge the details.

When the reporter had enough to get started, he turned off the recorder and the two men learned more about each other.

Patrick had grown up in Oregon and attended Oregon State University, majoring in Journalism. After graduation, finding a job was difficult at first, but finally signed on with the Salt Lake Tribune.

He and his partner Tim had been together for four years and live in a restored bungalow in the Avenues neighborhood by the state capital. He had no family near but had many friends he had met in Utah along the way.

Patrick turned the conversation to Jonah. Jonah had told him his very basics, but he wanted more. He told Patrick he would oblige as long as their private discussion wouldn't be in the article. Patrick agreed.

"Tell me all about Michelle."

Grateful for a chance to talk about her, Jonah's eyes smiled as he quipped, "She could be a royal pain in the butt. She was very competitive and since she was a natural athlete, she beat me at almost everything and didn't let up, but I wouldn't have wanted it any other way. She never put gas in the truck and often left it near empty when she drove it. She always seemed to have friends or even just acquaintances over even when I just wanted her to myself. Her dress-up clothes were khaki shorts and a t-shirt. I really miss all of those things."

Jonah took a drink. Being the trained interviewer he was, Patrick didn't speak during the momentary pause but waited for Jonah to return to the conversation.

"She was wonderful with people. She could make someone in a crowd feel they were the only one who mattered. She was a great listener. Maybe watching her is where I learned to listen.

"She always said that I was a good decision maker, and then grinned as she said my best decision was to marry her.

"You should've seen her around her students at the school. She would laugh and be silly with them at recess or cry with them when their parents divorced. We were constantly running into her former students who said she was their favorite teacher of all time. She would've been an amazing mother, if…

"I know it may be corny, but I felt she wasn't exactly a separate person in my life. Instead, she was an extension of me. And I was an extension of her.

"I really do miss all of those things. I think the worst part of her being gone is waking up in the morning and being reminded that it is true, it wasn't a dream. She won't be coming in to say, 'good morning, Sweetheart'.

Jonah raised his water glass to his lips. The beads of condensation on the glass dripped onto the tablecloth as he did. Condensation of a different kind formed in his eyes as he finished talking about the love of his life.

Patrick let his new friend sit for a minute then changed the conversation to Jonah's parents and siblings. He told the story of the trip with his brothers to the Pacific coast during high school. They both laughed until they almost teared up, the alcohol had loosened them up a little.

After some after-dinner small talk, they paid the tab and walked across the hot pavement to their cars. The day was giving them its approval with ample sunshine and a refreshing breeze.

"I'll start on the article tomorrow. I'll let you read it and have final approval before I print it. Get ready for more Fides."

Jonah reached out to shake his hand, but Patrick pulled him in for a hug. Though they had just met and separated in age by thirty years, they had quickly developed a friendship.

As Patrick drove off and merged into heavy traffic, Jonah sat in his car thinking for a while before heading home. He rarely got to talk about himself and tonight he had been the Fide. All the talk about Michelle brought back many more memories and unavoidable feelings. Sometimes the memories and feelings weighed too heavily on his soul. On some occasions, his heart broke so he wished he could rid himself of the memories. He knew, though, that he needed the good recollections even if they caused agony. In times such as this, Jonah couldn't help but realize how life is defined by the little moments and not grandiose accomplishments.

Arriving home, Wilhelm was happy to see him. Otherwise, the house was extra quiet and still. He became nostalgic thinking about their time dating and getting started in their married life.

Their quaint little rambler was missing her voice. The scent of her perfume was too long gone.

Chapter 16

Pastor Fide, Family Secret

After their great victory, Patrick returned to his office and Jonah reverted to the Fides waiting to reveal their secrets to him.

Currently, only one man was sitting on the bench. He appeared to be engrossed in the bible on his lap, but his glancing eyes showed he was easily being distracted.

Jonah motioned him over and asked loudly, "Did you want to talk to me?"

Looking at Jonah, the formally dressed black man stood up. His short-cut receding black hair brushed the leaves on the limb hanging above him.

As he walked toward Jonah's bench, he answered, "I think I do."

As he approached the Listening Bench, Jonah shook his hand and said, "Welcome to my bench, have a seat."

"I saw the flyer at the pavilion. I was very interested in what you do. I've never heard of anything like this before. I must say, I think there is a great need for this service."

His voice was powerful and deep, but soothing. The resonance had a James Earl Jones feel to it.

"Someone told me your name is Jonah, is that right?"

Jonah nodded.

He continued, "I'd prefer not to tell my name because of who I am."

"Actually, that is the way I prefer it also," Jonah replied.

"I've got something I've wanted to tell someone for a while now. When I saw what you on the bench and that you were African American as myself, I thought this might be the time."

"We may be the only two black men in this part of town," Jonah said with a grin.

The man laughed. "I know it used to be that way, but it's changing day by day and it's not as unusual now."

"I agree. I've been here thirty years and either it's gotten better, or I've just gotten used to it. Either way, I enjoy it here."

"Me too," he responded, "me too."

The small talk was over now it was time to get down to the business at hand. "What brings you here today? What do you want to tell me?"

"Let me start by assuring that this will be completely confidential. You'll see why in just a minute."

"I always keep things confidential. That's part of the whole premise."

"Good," he responded.

He was ready to reveal his situation. "Are you a religious man, Jonah?"

Jonah was caught off guard, but quickly recited the answer he had given many times in his life. "I'm not religious in any traditional sense. My family rarely went to church. I've only attended upon invitation and have no affiliation. But in the end, I do believe in a higher power. I feel there is someone, something in charge of the world as we know it. I'm just not prepared to commit to what it might be. I've always tried to live my life as if there is something. I hope there is an afterlife and since my wife died, I yearn for there to be an afterlife."

"That's a very honest answer, Jonah. I'm a pastor at a church in the valley. I moved here in 1990 after graduating from seminary in California. My father was a pastor before me, and I wanted to follow in his footsteps. I moved here as a youth minister after seminary and became head minister after a few years in the church.

"I love my position! I have some of the best parishioners you could imagine. They are practically family to me and my wife. I can't imagine doing anything to disappoint them.

"As much as I love what I'm doing and the people I work with, I carry a secret doubt. I'm not sure I believe anymore." The pastor dropped the heavy bomb into Jonah's lap.

"I'm not saying I don't believe in God. I do. I'm just saying I'm not sure I believe in the church itself, its doctrine, its policies, its dogma. Every Sunday, I feel I'm a hypocrite when I give a sermon. To feel genuine, I make sure my sermons are always about generic principles: love, faith, charity, and such.

"Please understand, Jonah, I have no desire to leave what I'm doing. I love counseling the individuals in the congregation and helping them through their trials. I love being part of our community outreach and offering charitable giving. I feel great about my actions day by day."

The Pastor was concluding. "I just needed someone to tell my deep feelings to. I obviously couldn't tell my dad or the church leaders over me. That's why I came to tell you."

His revelation was not shocking to Jonah. By now, he had heard such a variety of things that nothing surprised him even if he'd not heard a particular circumstance before.

Jonah responded to him in a very typical manner, "Are you glad you told me? Did it help you feel a sense of peace?"

The pastor thought for a few seconds and then replied, "Yes, Jonah, it did. Thank you for being here."

He stood up and walked toward Jonah at the other end of the bench. He gave a big hug and said, "God bless you, my brother! You're doing God's work, whoever that God is to you!"

"Thank you for dropping by, feel free to come back anytime."

Soon he was gone, lost amongst the park full of people dressed as he was, though, he still stood out.

The bench was also a place to reveal family secrets. One such occasion happened as the Pastor left and a lady probably in her early thirties approached the bench. The lady was visually stunning with all parts of her presentation intact. Even in the middle of a park, she radiated. She was probably five foot seven or eight. Her perfectly large chestnut curls fell in waves past her tan elegantly sloping shoulders. A sculpted nose took its perfect place beneath and between her hazel eyes. Her skin showed no blemish whether naturally so or skillfully concealed with perfect makeup.

"I want to be next to talk to you if that's ok," she asked.

"Of course, have a seat."

As she sat, her long legs were pivoted together and turned to one side with her hands properly in her lap as if being interviewed at a beauty pageant.

She spoke without hesitation hinting she had practiced this before. "I have a family secret that I don't believe anyone else knows. I have known it for twenty years and feel compelled to tell someone, but not just anyone. I can't let anyone else in my family find out about the secret, but it struggles within me to be released."

"That's what I'm here for. Whatever you tell me stays here."

"Good," she said, "I grew up here in the valley. I am the oldest of three kids. I have two younger brothers; Ted is two years younger, and Marcus is seven years younger. Marcus was a surprise to my parents. I think they thought they were through with just two children.

"When I was about eleven, some of my cousins and I were playing hide and seek at my uncle and aunt's house. During one of the turns, I found a great place to hide under a bed in one of my cousin's bedrooms.

"I hadn't been under the bed more than a minute when the door opened. I thought I would be caught immediately by the seeker, but the door closed quickly without the intruders leaving. I could see two pairs of feet. One pair was definitely my mom's. I recognized her shoes. The other feet were that of a man. When the man began talking, I recognized my uncle Bruce's voice. He was my dad's younger brother.

"Bruce spoke first, 'Marcus is getting so big. He's quite a handsome little boy.'

"Mom replied, 'Yes, as you know, he just turned five last month. He's a great kid.' There was something reserved in my mom's voice. It was as if she was uncomfortable with the conversation about her son.

"Uncle Bruce said, 'I can't believe Steve never has suspected anything. Has he?'.

"'No, at least he's never said anything to me. He just always assumed Marcus was his.'

"Even at eleven years old, I made the connection instantly. Bruce was Marcus' father!

"My mom continued, 'I don't even want to talk about it, Bruce. We should just leave it alone and never even speak to each other again about it. It was a mistake to be with you that one time. You knew I was in a vulnerable time in my marriage. You seduced me knowing I was weak.'

"Bruce said something like, 'As I remember, you were into it too, Kate. Have you ever told anyone?'

"Then Mom said, 'No, not even your brother. I can't believe he never made the connection or did the math. I can't stand the thought of telling anyone. I'm ashamed and I can't stand the idea of causing any rift between Marcus and his dad. I pray you will never reveal it, Bruce," Mom pleaded.

"'No, I won't. Steve's my brother and I wouldn't hurt him. I'm glad you two made it through the rough part of your marriage."

The lady on the bench continued her story to Jonah. "At this point, the seeker burst into the room looking for hiders. Mom and Uncle Bruce were certainly startled to be discovered and immediately left the room after the seeker said, 'Oh, excuse me' and left the room.

"I waited under the bed for a few minutes so as not to be discovered, then gingerly snuck out of the room, and ensured I was undetected. I went out behind the house and sat on a big landscaping rock with my back to the house. I tried to process the new information, crying as I did.

"Marcus was not my dad's son. My mom had been unfaithful. My little brother was my half-brother. This was so much for a young girl to process."

Her eyes began to redden. Jonah handed her a tissue.

"Thank you, sir. I made a promise to myself that I would never tell anyone, and I never have. I've not even told my husband. He has a tendency not to hold confidences.

"I could never look my uncle in the eye again. For the longest time, I didn't have a great relationship with my mom. Many years later, I did resolve it within myself and forgave her privately in my heart. I couldn't let that be a wedge between us forever.

"I worked extra hard to be good to Marcus. After all, it wasn't any fault of his. I always worried that he would find out and feel betrayed. I wanted to do everything I could to help his self-esteem in case he did ever discover the secret. As far as I know, he never has.

"You are the first and probably the last person I'll ever tell. It has burdened me so much, that I knew *somewhere*, *somehow*, I had to tell *someone*. You are that someone, I guess."

She then looked him in the eye, dabbed her wet eyes, and said, "Thank you for being here. I probably wouldn't ever have confided in anyone if you hadn't been doing this. I think you provide a service that the world needs. Sometimes we have things in our lives that we just can't tell those close to us."

"Yes, I've been finding that out. You are welcome."

With this, she gathered her things, walked over to Jonah, gave him a quick, but sincere hug, and said, "Thanks, again."

As she walked away, he was grateful that he could be her listening post. He felt once again very fulfilled in his newly found calling.

Chapter 17

The Coming Out Article

Patrick's article was perfect and humbling to Jonah. Jonah made a few suggestions before approving. The article was set to run on Thursday. If it was widely read, he expected to hear about it at the park on Monday. He decided to be at the park every day the next week, not just Monday, Wednesday, and Friday. He also decided to stay nine-to-five each day. He just prayed the weather would cooperate and he would feel up to it physically.

On Thursday, he checked the online version of the story. The title of the piece was, "The Listener in the Park". He read through the article, and it appeared pretty much as the advanced copy had. Later in the day,

Jonah received a few calls from acquaintances who had seen it. By Friday, the piece was being shared on social media. The public comments on the article were mostly positive, but some saw him as a voyeur of other people's problems. Some questioned his qualifications. Generally, though, people seemed to think it was a virtuous thing.

On Sunday, a television station reported the story. Patrick reached out to Jonah and told him they had contacted him to get Jonah's information for an interview. Jonah told him to hold off on giving his contact information until he saw the effect of the article.

The variety of Fides' stories was very interesting. In the short time he had been providing the service, he defined the topics of the confidences into five categories. Those categories were:

*Misdeeds done to others—affairs, cheating, lying—and the guilt associated.

*Regrets of choices made in lives—not following dreams, making bad choices—and the consequences that came.

*Lost love and loneliness.

*Secret actions from the past that affected society in general—treating people poorly, prejudices.

*Secret actions in the past that really affected no one, but the person still felt guilty—cheating on a test, lying.

An example of the last one came on the day the article came out. A cute little lady from a different time shuffled toward his bench. With silver hair precisely pinned up in a bun and a pantsuit from the Nixon era, she could've been anyone's grandma. Jonah supposed she was in her early eighties although it could've just been her osteoporosis stooping her and an arched back that gave that aged impression. As she got close enough for their eyes to meet, Jonah stood to welcome her. Lightly gripping her elbow into the palm of his hand, he helped lower her to the bench.

"Are you the one that listens to people's secrets?" she asked.

"I am. How are you today? Did you have something you wanted to tell me in confidence?"

Jonah noticed he was speaking louder than he normally did. Families near the lake were watching the whole process to make sure she was ok. He lowered his voice slightly to give her more privacy.

She cleared her throat. Taking a tissue from her purse and unfolding it meticulously, she spat a minuscule amount into it and dabbed the corners of her mouth. After placing the tissue back into her purse, she spoke, "Well, I understand that you are the one people come to tell secrets from their past." Apparently, she didn't remember she had just asked him a similar question.

"People come to me to tell all kinds of things. Is there something you want to tell?"

"Well," she started, "I have something that has weighed on me for years. It's hardly big enough to go to my priest for, but it's something I want to tell someone and get off my conscience."

"I'd love to be the one you tell. Go ahead when you are ready."

"When I was in my early twenties, I loved to read. I still do, but it's much harder now with my cataracts and such.

"In my early life, we didn't have a lot of money to buy books, so most of my books were checked out from the city library. This was in the early sixties and a lot of good books were being written. Not like the trash that they are putting out today."

He grinned.

"Well, about ten years after this time, I was doing some spring cleaning and I came across four books from the library that I had never returned. Oh my! I was horrorstruck! I had checked out these books a decade before."

Her dramatic regret was adorable to Jonah.

She continued, "Well, I took those books, got in my Chevy Impala and drove down to the library, dropped the books off in the slot for book returns, and drove home relieved that I had gotten them back to their proper owner."

"Here is the kicker, though. I never paid the ten years of fines that must've accrued."

Oh, the horror!! She was looking straight into his eyes as if she were telling him she was part of the Great Brinks Robbery of the 1950s.

"For years, I expected the police to knock on my door at any time and take me away in handcuffs in front of all my neighbors. I could've just gone and paid it, but I was too embarrassed. Over time, I just lived with the guilt but never told anyone. I made a pact with myself that I would never do a dishonest thing again and think I've succeeded.

"What do you think I should do?" She ended with anticipation of what he would say.

Normally, Jonah didn't give advice. He wasn't a social worker or a priest, so he didn't venture down that path. In this case, he felt it would be harmless.

He suggested, "Ma'am, I don't think you need to carry this burden anymore. Your great life of honesty since the event is atonement enough and you have made the world a better place because of it."

Jonah felt as if he were a priest saying, go and sin no more, but of course, he wasn't.

She didn't respond immediately. She collected her things and warily stood. Still facing the bench, she turned to him and said, "Thank you, friend. I feel I can leave that burden here with you. I don't have to carry it with me anymore."

As they said their goodbyes, he could see there was no one else waiting so he stood and stretched. He was chuckling a little still thinking about her great iniquity.

Jonah's thoughts turned a little more reflective. To this sweet octogenarian, her actions had been weighing on her as heavily over the years as someone who tells him of an affair or how they wronged their employer. She had been carrying this weight for fifty years. Her action may have been benign, but her guilt was malignant. He realized discounting her feelings was not appropriate. If the world could feel guilt over seemingly inconsequential acts as this, society would be in a better place. Reflecting on her visit made him want to be a better person.

On Monday following Patrick's piece on the paper's website, Jonah was anxious and a little apprehensive about what would happen. He got to his bench earlier than usual. A homeless man had slept on the bench the previous night and was just leaving. Jonah helped the man get his belongings together and gave him a ten-dollar bill—which was all the cash he had.

Jonah left Wilhelm at home this day. He was leaving his dog more often as things got busier on the bench. He tried to make it up to him most afternoons by taking him for a walk around their neighborhood.

Exactly at nine o'clock, the first Fide appeared. He was about Jonah's age. After strolling casually up to the bench, he said, "I saw the thing on the Tribune's website about you. I thought I would get here early in case you were busy. I've got to be to work by ten."

"Well, you're my first of the day. Have a seat." Jonah enthusiastically offered.

Jonah's enthusiasm was because not only was this the first Fide of the post-article era, but the man had a natural positivity that he carried with him. The man had very light skin and tight blonde natural curls. His light skin revealed several small sun-kissed freckles over the bridge of his average nose.

His energy was naturally high-strung and as soon as he sat down, he began his story. "Jonah, my name is Mark. I know your name because of the article. My reason for being here is not necessarily confidential, I just needed someone to open up to about my life and career or maybe I should say *careers*."

"Of course, Mark. Go ahead."

"I've been an entrepreneur long before I could pronounce the word or knew what it meant. As a boy, I mowed yards and walked dogs in my neighborhood all to make my own money. My mom and dad owned a donut shop and I guess it was in my blood.

As I got older, I knew I wanted nothing more than to be in business for myself. I wanted, though, to be more successful than my parents had. They worked long hours in the donut shop and never seemed to have enough money. I will say, though, that they always seemed happy. My goal was to not only own my own successful business but to be independently wealthy.

"I dropped out of college after my first year. I was anxious to start life's journey sooner than later.

"I spent the next fifteen years chasing a dream in multi-level marketing. I was the guy who was constantly harassing my friends to let me come into their house and tell them about my special opportunity. I went from one 'best opportunity of a lifetime' to another a couple of times per year. I don't remember exactly how many of them I joined. Some I even started.

"Because I was always promising my new recruits that they could be almost instant millionaires, I had to live the part for them to see. I leased cars I couldn't afford and lived in houses that bankrupted us, twice in twenty years. Every time I started a new venture that was certainly going to make us rich, I put in crazy hours. I justified the time away from my family, by telling myself and my wife that once we made it, I would have all the time in the world to spend with them because my downline would be paying us so well."

Jonah wondered when the man was going to take a breath. At this rate, he wouldn't have trouble getting to work by ten because he would finish telling his life story by nine-fifteen.

He continued, "after fifteen years and who knows how many failed network marketing ventures, I realized that this was never going to work for me.

"It was a hard reality for me. I spent the next several years searching out other business opportunities. Because I was nowhere near where I wanted to be in life, I felt even more pressure to find something that made piles of money, quickly. Even when a new venture started making money, if it wasn't an insane amount, I would sell it for a bargain price and move on to something else.

"My wife was very patient…for a while, but then started to encourage and then beg for me to find something solid and settle down even if it didn't make us rich. She repeatedly reminded me that our kids needed time with their father. I rationalized by saying that I may not be giving them quantity time, but I was giving them quality time. She got so annoyed at hearing this, that one time she burst out, 'It's not quality time they need, it's just TIME!'

"Jonah, I never took her advice. This year, my last child went off to college in Arizona. After that, I looked at my wife in our empty nest and finally realized what she was talking about. In chasing my riches, I had lost my opportunity to spend adequate time with my greatest treasures—my wife and children. Along the way, I had not developed the relationship with my wife that we will need to enjoy being empty nesters. I looked at her and realized I didn't really know her."

For the first time, Mark stopped his narrative. He looked down at the ground, took a deep breath, and spoke philosophically.

"In the last little while, I've been sobered by some reality that I would've been wise to realize a long time ago.

"Success in life is not about how many great things we begin, but by how many average things we complete. It's easy to say at the beginning of a project, 'look at me, I'm going to be so very successful', but it's another thing in a year to be able to show my success or lack of it. In chasing my dreams, I crapped on the needs of my wife and kids. They didn't need a rich husband and dad; they simply needed a husband and dad who was there.

"It's true what they say that we only get one life to live. I'm pretty sure I messed mine up."

Fearing there wouldn't be another gap in his spewing, Jonah immediately jumped in with a reply. "Who says we only have one life? I certainly don't believe so. I just recently retired and then tragically lost my wife. The way I see it, that was my first life, and it was wonderful. Now, I've got to reinvent myself in whatever time I have left. I know my sweet wife would've wanted it that way. We certainly all have regrets, Mark. You can't change what has been done, but you can impact what happens from this day on. Why don't you consider starting a new life? Surprise your wife and kids with the new Mark."

"I know," he replied, "I just have lost so much."

For the first time at the bench, the man paused. The deafening pause was needed for him to collect his thoughts and reflect on Jonah's words. During those short moments, he formulated a plan. He didn't know the details yet, but he was resolute on the first steps.

Mark stood up, looked directly at Jonah, and said, "thank you, Jonah. Telling my story out loud and your words of wisdom have motivated me to make a change. Ever since my realization of how I've screwed up, I knew I needed to change, but telling you has put it out in the universe and now I feel the power to make a difference. I'm not going to the office today. I'm turning around and going to get my wife from her job and spend the day doing nothing but be with her. My change has to start today. I don't have forever left."

The two men shook hands and Jonah wished him well. As he walked away toward the waiting bench, Jonah could see three individuals waiting there to talk to him. The article had worked. Throughout the day, he had a steady stream of Fides. He saw many potential clients leave, not able to wait. The article had performed much better than ever expected. Now, he worried about all the disappointed people who had to walk away. He immediately thought of Marvin and Pam and how they could be wonderful assistants.

Randy Judd

Chapter 18

A Second Chance at Love

Since the newspaper article, the stream of Fides increased from a trickle to a flow. After listening to several people in the morning and taking a brief lunch in his car, the next Fide to come to the Listening Bench was a man in his thirties. The man's head was topped with red hair, a fair complexion, and a slightly protruding belly. Jonah greeted him, then motioned for him to sit down. He went through his quick list of disclaimers and how this whole process works —he had the spiel down to about twenty seconds.

His usual opener had become, "what would you like to confide in me today?"

"I wanted to tell someone about how I screwed up a great chance at love in my life," he began.

Lost romance was not an unusual topic at the Listening Bench. Jonah was beginning to believe there were more lonely people in the world than he had ever imagined. "Go on, whenever you are ready."

"I have never dated much in my life, so when I finally found someone who seemed interested in me, I was ecstatic. This happened about two or three years ago. We got really close, really fast. She was great. I knew she cared about me, and I cared immensely for her. After a few months, she wanted more of a commitment from me than I was ready to give. At least more than I thought I was ready to give. Looking back, I made a big mistake not to tell her right then how I felt, but seldom having been in love before, I was afraid.

"Anyway, she got mad at me and questioned my love for her. That hurt me because I felt stronger for her than I ever had anyone before. She left the next day for a wedding somewhere back in the Midwest.

"A day or so after that, my brother called me from England to tell me that Mum's cancer had returned, and she didn't have long to live. I reluctantly quit my IT job and flew back to England to be with her.

Because my phone had been the property of my employer, I turned my phone in when I left. Everything had happened so quickly. I hadn't gotten my contact information before I turned it in, so I lost her phone number.

"I didn't think I would be in England for too long, but as Mum's illness dragged on, I took a job in London and stayed there through her death. I just recently returned to America. I made a feeble attempt to reach out to Pam, but I chickened out knowing she had probably moved on by now and my leaving probably made her think less of me anyway."

"Leaving her is one of the great regrets of my life. I feel I may have missed out on the best chance at love that I will ever have."

Something about his story was sounding familiar, but when he said the name Pam, Jonah knew it had to be the same. His friend and park mate, Pam had told him a similar story while running in the park at the beginning of all this. She was the reason he got into the confiding game.

Because Jonah took confidentiality as a sacred trust, he couldn't say anything to this young man about Pam or vice versa. Knowing they both yearned for the same thing, he knew he had to devise a way to get them together.

Jonah let the man complete his story even though Jonah's mind was engaged in planning and not in what the man was saying.

"Can I ask you an odd question?" Jonah generally didn't ask questions, but he had to this time to put his plan into action. He knew that Pam ran on Fridays like clockwork. "I know this sounds strange, and I can't tell you why I'm requesting this, but could come back and see me at nine o'clock tomorrow morning?"

The question was odd, and Oliver wasn't sure about it. "Why?"

"As I said, I can't say exactly, but it is important that you come back." Jonah could still see he wasn't convinced. "I'll tell you what, if you come back and it's a disappointment, I'll give you a hundred-dollar bill."

Being a man who was trying to get his life back, this convinced him. "Well, if it's so important, I guess I can. By the way, I know you said we didn't need to know each other's names, but my name is Oliver."

Jonah was giddy. "Nice to meet you, Oliver. I look forward to tomorrow morning." And he did! "Just stand over beside the waiting bench when you get here."

As he left, Jonah couldn't help but think this could go terribly wrong, but he had to break the listener's code and give love a chance to rekindle.

Friday morning, he came early. He knew Pam usually arrived before he did, so he wanted to catch her before nine. Happily, as expected, Jonah saw Pam at about eight forty and flagged her down.

"Hey, Jonah, what's up?"

He had walked quickly to meet her and was slightly out of breath. "I've got an odd favor to ask of you."

"Ok, what's that?"

"Could you meet me at the waiting bench in about twenty to thirty minutes? It's really important," he explained.

"I guess so. Can I ask what this is about?" she hesitantly asked.

"I can't tell you right now, but I can tell you it's not something bad."

She was glad for the assurance. Her first thought was that someone they mutually knew from the park had died or was sick.

"Ok, I'll be back in a few." She jogged off bewildered.

As nine o'clock neared, he sat in the usual location on his bench. Wilhelm was not with him today. There was one person with him on the listening bench. Soon, Jonah saw Oliver walk up to the waiting bench. Oliver looked his way and when they had eye contact, Jonah held up one finger as if to signal that he would be with him in one minute.

As another moment passed, Pam came down the path. Jonah watched her intently. He didn't know how all of this would go down, so he was riveted to watching over the shoulder of the person talking to him on the bench. He also gave her the one-minute finger when she stood by the bench.

Neither of them looked directly at the other. Other people were walking on the sidewalks, so there was a bit of hubbub around them. Jonah saw the first light of recognition from Pam. She glanced at Oliver, then stared a little more. Jonah had no doubt she recognized Oliver and was processing the situation.

As if her stare tapped him on the shoulder, Oliver glanced up at the girl standing a few feet behind the other end of the bench. When their eyes met, they stood for a moment, assuring themselves of what they were seeing. The two former lovers didn't run flowingly into each other's arms as in a Hallmark movie. They did smile and walk cautiously toward each other, paused a minute for some reconciliation greeting, and then hugged. It wasn't a romantic hug, but the type of hug you give some acquaintance you haven't seen in a while. They talked just for a minute. Of course, Jonah couldn't hear what was being said, but they both turned to look at him simultaneously. He gave them a wave and two thumbs up. He could see them walk to another bench and sit to talk. They rested in the shade on the bench for a couple of hours, but Jonah lost track of them as he listened to other people's stories.

A couple of days passed since the reunion when they caught up with Jonah. Things were going well. There had been a substantial gap in their relationship so neither was rushing the bond. Jonah periodically received updates from Pam in the park. Then, a few months later, she handed him an envelope containing their wedding announcement. Jonah choked up knowing that he had helped their lost love be reunited. If able, he would definitely attend. In this moment, he missed Michelle profoundly.

Randy Judd

Chapter 19

Patrick's News

The first few weeks after the article were more productive than anyone expected. There were many more Fides than Jonah could possibly accommodate. He was excited when both Pam—Fide number two— and Marvin—Fide number one— agreed to help a few shifts a week. They had been helping along the way when Jonah couldn't make it, and frankly, he felt they did as good of a job as he did. There was no right or wrong way.

He was very encouraged that Marvin had taken to the task so well. He filled in for Jonah when there were doctors' appointments, or he simply didn't feel well. Marvin found purpose in his own life doing this alongside Jonah. Overall, Marvin appeared happier lately. Jonah was very pleased to see this. After all, he was a genuinely good man and Jonah was sure he was a good listener to the people on the benches.

In about three weeks, the pace slowed somewhat. The flow became manageable. By this time, Jonah had listened to hundreds of people. He felt he was doing something great for humanity and providing a service to mankind. He knew Michelle would've been —was—proud of him.

One theme that was more prevalent than any others was loneliness.

Jonah was extremely delighted one afternoon to see Veronica— Michelle's best friend—come to the bench when no one else was around. He hadn't talked to Verny since Michelle's funeral. It was good to see her. They talked about the past and Michelle. Neither of them could hold back tears—but that was ok. There is no apology needed in grief.

"Veronica, what are you doing here today?" he casually asked.

She responded, "I actually came to see you, believe it or not. I saw the story about you on TV and I thought I would come by and see if you would listen to me for a bit."

He stammered a bit, "I've never listened to anyone I've known, but if you feel you want to talk so let's have a seat."

Having come straight from school, she was dressed nicely. She swept off the bench with her hand before she sat. Jonah had never thought Veronica was an attractive woman, but she was actually aging nicely and carried herself confidently. For the first time, he saw her in a different light than he had before. She was a very, very good woman. He loved her pure soul. She had been part of their family over the years.

She began, "Of course you know, I haven't been lucky in love during my entire lifetime."

To contradict her would've been insulting. She knew that he knew her story.

"When it comes right down to it, I'm ok. I'm happy with myself, my career, and my family. I'm productive and volunteer in the community.

"But when we lost Michelle, a part of me died with her. I didn't realize how much of my being was occupied by her spirit."

That was a perfect way to describe Michelle's absence. He understood completely.

"I know it's coming up on a year since she was taken, but I'm really missing her."

Her reddened eyes were again producing tears. Fortunately, she had her own tissues and Jonah gave her time to dab them away and compose herself.

She continued, "I find my life has a huge void and I don't know what to do to fill it. I can't just get another friend of thirty years. I want to date again, but not to lead to marriage. I'm pretty set in my ways. I just want a good man to be with. Someone who can hold me when I cry and laugh with or at me when I do dumb stuff. Someone to look forward to seeing at the end of the day."

To Veronica, he was not the man of the Listening Bench, and she was not one of his Fides. She was a dear friend, so he slid to the other end of the bench, put his arm around her, and let her cry, consoling her for several minutes without dialogue.

He noticed a person standing at the waiting bench. He told Verny that he would be right back and went to the lady at the other bench.

"I'm going to be a while here—would you mind going to the bench over on the other side?" Jonah pointed through the trees to the bench where Marvin was visiting with people. "That man's name is Marvin, and he is a great listener." She was disappointed but wasn't put off too much.

Jonah returned to his bench and returned to the other end from Verny in his normal position. "I'm so sorry, especially in such a crucial place in your story, but I knew I wanted to spend as much time with you as needed."

"I know exactly how you feel. I guess that's not really a fair statement. None of us knows exactly how another feels, but I think the magnitude of our feelings is the same, wouldn't you agree?"

She nodded. They reminisced about Michelle for several minutes. This helped slow the crying. They shared experiences of her that made them laugh. They talked about her caring actions. They even laughed at some of her frailties. For a brief moment, Michelle was there with them.

During a pause in the conversation as they both gazed off in memories of her, he glanced over to Marvin's bench to see if the lady had gotten taken care of adequately. At that point, the idea came to him. Maybe it was serendipity or maybe it was Michelle's loving inspiration, but Jonah felt driven to act on his intuition.

"Veronica, I know this may be awkward and I totally get that it's coming out of nowhere, but what if I knew a man that I could introduce you to? I'm not talking about a random setup, but a man who I've come to know who has a sweetness about him that you could appreciate. He's been single for a long time too, but I've gotten to know him well and I think you two would be good for each other."

She looked bewildered and hesitant. This wasn't what she came here for, but he could see hope in her eyes. "Who is he?"

Jonah asked her to turn, and he pointed out Marvin. She watched from a distance as he talked to the lady on his bench. She watched for a minute or two, her eyes dilated with interest.

"I suppose you could introduce us, but no more than an introduction for now," she agreed.

"Of course not, just an introduction."

After the lady left Marvin's bench, Jonah and Veronica approached him.

Jonah announced their approach. "Hey Marvin, I want you to meet someone."

Marvin turned toward them and stood up and offered his hand. "Hi, I'm Marvin."

Jonah continued. "This is Veronica Nichols. She was Michelle's best friend. She dropped by today to see me."

Veronica grasped his hand and only Jonah could see that they lingered holding hands a little longer than normal.

"It's a pleasure to meet you, Veronica."

"You too, Marvin."

Jonah jumped in, "I need to run to my truck for a minute and didn't want to leave her sitting by herself. Would you mind hanging out with her for a few minutes?"

Jonah knew it wasn't his smoothest move, but it worked. As he returned from his truck after an extended ten minutes, he could see them actively engaged in a conversation. Both were smiling, gesturing, and feeling at ease.

The following day, each of them called him to get contact information for the other. They went on their first date the following weekend.

Jonah went home to his empty house knowing that Michelle was happy with his actions. He wanted to be with her so badly. He understood everything Veronica was saying about missing Michelle. He did have hope that the hurt would lessen in the near future.

As he was winding down from a consistent stream of Fides with diverse stories to tell, Jonah got a text from Patrick. *Give me a call when you can talk a little.*

They had been talking once a week or so since they became friends, so he wasn't surprised or rushed. After finishing cleaning up his area and walking to his truck, he inserted his earbuds and called.

"Hello, Jonah. How's your day been?"

"It was pretty busy, not the busiest, but I helped a lot of people, I think."

He moved on to the reason for the call. "Hey, I wanted to talk to you about something somewhat serious."

Jonah was intrigued. "Oh? Go ahead."

Patrick continued, "I heard a rumor from one of the reporters at the crime desk that you were being investigated for what you are doing down there."

"What?" He said, incredulously.

"I know," he replied, "I was shocked too."

"Was I supposed to get a license or something since I take up so much of the park? I mean its public property, right?"

He answered, "No, it seems to be more serious than that."

There was a brief pause as Jonah stepped up into his truck and settled in for the call. "Well, what can it possibly be?"

"I don't know all the details, so I'm going to do a little digging," he replied, "but what I understand is there is some question about if you are practicing medicine without a license!"

"Oh, that's ludicrous!" He replied, shaking his head. "All I'm doing is listening to people."

"I guess my article raised the awareness of some in the therapy community. At the least, they are thinking you are practicing therapy without a license.

"Now, don't get too worried yet. I'll follow up with some of my contacts to see who is investigating it and what their intention is."

They finished up the conversation. "Ok, let me know as soon as you learn any more. Thanks for telling me."

Patrick agreed to keep him updated.

As Jonah drove out of the park, he wasn't concerned. He knew if they did investigate, they would see that he wasn't doing anything except helping people to be heard.

Jonah felt inspired to do something different this evening. Even though the sun was setting earlier in the day, he still had time to drive up into the canyons and take a hike. The gold leaves of the Autumn Aspens swirled around his truck as he wound his way up into the forest. After parking at the trailhead, he laced up his hiking boots and grabbed the carbon fiber walking pole that Michelle had given him after his leg had healed. The fall wind was little more than a breeze but caused him to zip his light jacket for a little extra comfort. He then followed the trail into the gilded trees. Hiking had become much harder for him, so he chose a trail with very little undulation or incline.

With his days filled with conversation, he found himself needing solitude and silence. There was no better way to get that tranquil recharge than this.

He would've given up all the tranquility for the rest of his life to have Michelle beside him, but she wasn't. If he followed his agnostic friends' beliefs, she never would be. That thought hurt too much, so he retained a certain level of hope and yearning. As Jonah had grown older, he was more and more open to the idea of an afterlife – whatever that was. Even though it wasn't in his core, he ached for it to be true on some level.

Recently he was in a discussion with that agnostic friend. The friend firmly stood by his belief that when people die, they cease to exist. Jonah understood the man's beliefs since he had been somewhat of that belief most of his own life, but lately, he had started to believe that there was no harm in having some hope. Jonah ended their discussion by quoting Pascal:

'Let us weigh the gain and the loss in wagering that God is. Let us estimate these two chances. If you gain, you gain all; if you lose, you lose nothing. Wager, then, without hesitation that He is.'

His friend didn't argue with that.

After a mile into the woods, Jonah turned around and headed back to the trailhead. He didn't want to get stuck out after dark. It had been a beautiful time to be alone with his thoughts and he certainly had a lot to think about.

By the time he got back to the parking lot, he was fatigued. It was becoming harder and harder to do the things he and Michelle had always loved.

Randy Judd

Chapter 20

Justifying Himself

I t took a couple of days to hear back from Patrick. Jonah assumed this was a good sign. No news is good news, as they say. That wasn't true in this case.

He called Jonah early in the morning a few days later. Jonah was sitting at his kitchen table with his computer open. Wilhelm had settled into his doggy bed after their walk. His dog was certainly showing his age too and spent much of the day in his bed. Jonah rarely took his companion to the park anymore because days were always long, and he deserved to be comfortable at home. He did try to take his dog and dear friend on a walk whenever he could.

"Well, I've got some news and it's not necessarily good," Patrick jumped right in.

"The Salt Lake Police Department is doing an investigation at the request of the Utah Medical Guild."

"Ok?" was all Jonah could come up with during the pause.

"They've actually already sent an undercover agent to visit with you. I think you can expect a visit from detectives within a week." He paused to give Jonah a chance to process.

Jonah jumped in during the pause. "Well, this is just stupid! I'm just a guy sitting on a bench listening to people tell their woes. It's not as if I'm doing kidney transplants or giving them meds!"

He wasn't shaken. He wasn't even really mad. He was just incredulous at the ludicrousy of the whole thing.

"Thanks Patrick, for letting me know all of this. I guess I'll just go back to my bench today and keep my eye open for Brisco and Green from *Law and Order* to stroll up to me. I know it must be a high priority on their docket." His sarcasm could be cut with a police-issued tactical knife.

It was hard to not be distracted that day at the park, but nothing happened. Jonah started viewing each Fide as a potential undercover agent. He tried to think back over the last couple of weeks as to who the fake Fide could've been. There had been too many for him to consider.

About a week after the warning conversation with Patrick, they came.

They came as he was just finishing the day and heading to his truck. In the middle of summer, it's unusual to see two men in long pants and collared shirts walking through the park. Jonah knew who they were immediately.

Not wanting to get Patrick in trouble for his digging on his behalf, Jonah played dumb. He gave a nod as he approached them on the sidewalk but didn't slow his pace.

Both detectives were probably in their forties. One was white, the other was darker, probably Pacific Islander, he thought. They seemed like pretty nice men, the kind of guys who would be buying fishing gear down at one of his sporting goods stores.

"Excuse me," the darker man said, "are you, Jonah Freeman?"

Jonah stopped a few feet from them. "Well, yes, I am. What can I do for you gentlemen?" He was playing the ruse well.

"I'm Detective Armstrong and this is Detective Garrett." He subsequently reached out his hand to shake. Jonah obliged and then shook Garrett's hand also.

"We're from the Salt Lake Police Department," he continued, "we need to talk to you, Mr. Freeman. Can you come with us to the department to talk?"

Continuing his act, Jonah said what anyone would say, "What's this about?"

Garrett chimed in, "We are in the middle of an investigation that we think you can help us with."

"What investigation?" The thespian in him questioned.

"We'll tell you down at the station. Can you meet us there?"

Wanting to keep everyone on his side, Jonah agreed.

As he drove to the station a mile or so away, Jonah wondered how this was going to play out. He didn't think they would be putting him on the ground with handcuffs for such a benign potential crime. In the back of his head, he could remember his dad telling him what to do in the presence of the police. Hopefully, a black man in his fifties would not cause them much concern. He was happy that one of the detectives, at least, had some color in him.

When Jonah arrived at the department's offices, the daytime employees were going home for the day. Without the administrative and other daytime workers, the offices were quiet and cavernous. The detectives escorted him into an interrogation room. The room honestly didn't appear as anything he had seen on *Dateline*. It must've been nicer than the ones they interview murderers and rapists. The furniture was plain but newer. There was a scent of freshly installed carpeting. Jonah had always enjoyed that smell.

Feigning shock, Jonah asked, "What could I possibly know that would help what you're investigating?"

"Well, Jonah...can I call you Jonah?"

He nodded.

"We've been contacted by the Utah Medical Guild concerning what you are doing at the park." That made it sound as if Jonah was a flasher or something. "They seem to consider it practicing medicine without a license. Not exactly practicing medicine, but more as though you're practicing therapy without a therapist's license."

Jonah responded with some of his practiced lines, "I didn't think I needed a license to listen to others in a park. People do that every day!"

Armstrong took his turn, "But they don't advertise it and give advice to people they don't even know."

He hadn't practiced for this. "Look, I don't give advice. I just listen to people tell me their stories."

Garrett spoke, "As part of our investigation, we sent an undercover agent to visit you. At the end of the visit, she was undecided about if you had given advice or not. It wasn't completely clear, but for the sake of caution, we decided to move forward."

Armstrong had previously been standing. He sat down across the table. "Jonah, to tell you the truth, I don't know much about the law on this type of case, it only happens every couple of years, but I'm trying to learn."

Jonah was happy that both detectives treated him with a great deal of respect. They weren't condescending or belligerent. They almost had the attitude of, *we don't know exactly why we are doing this, but we have to do our job.*

Armstrong set a bottled water next to him—he'd seen enough crime shows to think this might be a ploy to get his DNA. But seriously...

Armstrong continued, "These kinds of cases don't come up often. When they do, they are brought to the District Attorney's office, and they send it back to us to investigate. Since none of us knows much about the medical world, the D.A. turns to the Utah Medical Guild and asks them to do an investigation of their own. It's kind of their own trial to determine the facts. After they are through, they give a report and recommendation to the D.A. Although the D.A. is not bound by what the guild finds, they usually follow the guild's advice and decide whether to charge and try the case."

"So, are you saying I'm going to be tried by a bunch of doctors?" Jonah asked.

"Well, it's not a trial exactly and they will proceed with or without you, but it is certainly in your best interest to be there. The guild will let you know the time and place. You can have an attorney with you if you want, but they have no legal standing in this procedure."

There was a pause. Jonah broke the silence, "So, am I under arrest?"

"Oh no, not at all," Garret answered, "we are still in the investigation stage. You are free to go about living your life as you see fit."

"Within the law!" Armstrong quipped. Detective humor, he guessed.

Randy Judd

Chapter 21

Before the Guild

Jonah received notice of the hearing delivered by a constable to his house. Wilhelm raised his head to see who was coming up the steps, but laid it back down, too tired for the trouble.

The date was set for the following Thursday, a little over a week away. This was good. Jonah didn't want this nonsense to stretch out too long.

At the park, he talked to both Pam and Marvin about covering for him on that day. People were disappointed not to get to talk to THE Listener, but his two friends represented the bench well when asked, especially Marvin who jumped at the opportunity.

The days clicked away and soon the appointed day for the hearing arrived. Jonah had not considered an attorney. He wasn't about to pay three hundred dollars an hour for an attorney to sit there not being able to have input.

The hearing was held in a boardroom at the Salt Lake County courthouse. He had assumed it would be in a courtroom, but as he had been told, this wasn't a trial, simply a hearing to determine whether the district attorney should proceed with charges.

Jonah stepped through the right side of the double doors into the boardroom as a clerical person exited the other door. Stopping at the head of the table, he could see three official-looking people—one woman, two men—at the other end of the table. He had to assume they were the ones who would be conducting the inquisition. The woman and one of the men were dressed smartly in business attire. The other man, for some reason, had on what could only be described as a formal lab coat. With his lab coat, he had on a tie and a name tag. Jonah thought maybe the doctor had the lab coat on in case there was surgery that needed to be performed on the table in the middle of the meeting. Those three officials at the head of the table were busy shuffling papers and talking amongst themselves.

The man in the lab coat looked up and called to Jonah. "Mr. Freeman, I presume?" When he nodded, the man continued, "you may have a seat at that end, and we'll get started shortly."

There were a couple of administrative people at the sides of the table and another lady who looked familiar, but he could not remember from where.

He took his place at the end of the twenty-foot table. The scene reminded him of pictures he'd seen recently of Vladimir Putin of Russia. With Putin, it was certainly a power play when his guests were sometimes forty feet away. Jonah guessed these people had been assigned the room randomly, so they weren't being Putin-esque.

Jonah's attire was a step up from his Liberty Park attire. He was wearing black slacks and a dull pink polo shirt. Michelle always encourage him to wear pink. He was ok with how he looked also.

Sitting down, Jonah felt conspicuous. No one was interacting with him and as typical, everyone was on their phone. He, of course, checked his too, though he rarely received messages.

After about ten minutes of sitting and exactly at the appointed hour, the woman stayed standing while everyone else took their seats.

"Good morning, everyone, I'm Doctor Elizabeth Ventura, head of Psychiatric Research at the University of Utah. I will be conducting this hearing. I am joined by Dr. Jonathon Pratt (Lab Coat Man) and Dr. Miguel Sanchez, the President of the Guild. Dr. Sanchez has asked me to conduct this hearing.

"Procedurally, you'll notice that we have three microphones on the table, one on our end, one in front of Mr. Freeman, and a portable one in the middle. This is to help with the recording of the meeting."

Jonah pulled his microphone closer so he could speak right into it. He didn't want there to be any ambiguity in what he was saying.

At this point, Doctor Ventura took her seat. Her microphone was directly in front of her. "We are here today to determine if the Utah Medical Guild should recommend that Jonah Freeman be indicted for practicing medicine without a license." She nodded to Jonah. There were no formal introductions made of him or the rest of the people in the room.

"Mr. Freeman, thank you for coming. You are not required to be here, but we certainly appreciate it." She feigned sincerity.

For about twenty minutes, she continued reading from a document about the procedures they would be following, and the laws referenced. One would think that he would've taken it more seriously, but Jonah zoned out a few times during the explanations.

"Mister Freeman, do you have any questions before proceeding?"

"I don't, no ma'am."

"Please address me as Doctor Ventura. I can assure you I've earned it."

"Yes, ma'am." His defiance was not hidden well.

After some more legalities, reading the allegations and the law pertaining, it was time for Jonah to be part of the proceedings.

"Mr. Freeman, a few questions to start. Can you give us your background —schooling, professional training, et cetera?"

His answers were quick. He suspected he knew where she was going.

She continued, "What, if any, medical training do you have?"

Jonah replied, "I'm CPR certified. Does that count?"

Dr. Ventura was annoyed. "Mr. Freeman, do you think this procedure is a joke?"

He leaned forward to speak directly into the microphone, "Yes. Yes Ma'am, I do." There he went again. He just couldn't seem to help himself.

"Mr. Freeman, you are not required to be here, and we are not required to have you here, but if you want to have a say in the matter, I suggest you take this seriously. The outcome could be pretty consequential for you."

"I understand. I will try to hold my contempt. Thank you for allowing me to present my side."

With her small victory, Dr. Ventura continued, "Have you ever been to a therapist or know how they practice?"

"I have had experiences with therapists and psychiatrists in the past but know nothing about their day-to-day procedures."

She continued, "Tell us about what you do in the park, how it began, how long you've been doing it, and so forth."

Jonah recited the origins of the Listening Bench. He took the group through the growth and the number of people served, especially after

Patrick's article. He talked about the process in general and how the interaction goes.

"Do you give these individuals advice about how they should proceed?" The first probing question.

"The people do not come to the bench for advice, generally. They just come to be heard."

"You said, generally. Are there times when they want advice?"

He responded, "Sure, sometimes. If this happens, I tell them what I would do in their circumstance or ask them a series of questions to lead them to their own answers."

There was a pause as Dr. Ventura turned to her colleagues. With hands held to the sides of their mouths, only a mumble could be heard at Jonah's end of the table. This went on for two or three minutes, but it seemed longer. She turned her attention back to him, straightened the papers in her hand by rapping them on the table, then continued.

"Sir, do you feel qualified in giving these people advice?"

He quickly answered, "No, I do not. Let me remind you that I said sometimes I talk to them further, but it is not a general circumstance. If I do tell them what I would do or lead them to their own answers, it's based on my life experience and only that. I am not qualified to give them anything past that."

"Our hearing here today is to see if your actions led these people to assume you are an expert and therefore, the advice you give is seen as expert advice.

"Let me put it this way, Mr. Freeman. When you go to your doctor, do you take their advice because they are experts in their field and have been properly trained?"

Jonah thought for a moment and responded, "Of course I do. I know that they have much more knowledge than I have, at least about medicine. I respect the years of training they have. I do, however, have a different way I approach my health. I consider my doctors to be consultants—they tell me what I should do, and I decide whether I will do it."

Doctor Pratt was obviously bothered by this statement. He shifted in his seat, slightly shook his head, and made some kind of grunt signifying his displeasure with Jonah's statement.

"I do not have disdain for doctors. In fact, I have a great deal of respect for my family doctor and the specialists I am currently seeing. I feel they stay current on research and give great recommendations. In the end, though, I am the one who decides to follow their advice and possibly reap the consequences. I should point out that I do have an issue respecting arrogance."

This line of questioning went on for about an hour before Dr. Ventura seemed satisfied for the time and took the hearing in a different direction.

Looking at some notes in front of her, she spoke, "We would now request to hear from Detective Nancy Jackman of the Salt Lake Police Department. Detective Jackman visited Jonah undercover as a person needing to be helped."

Now Jonah knew where he had seen her. With as many people who come to the bench, he rarely remembers particular stories told, but he can often recognize the people who sit at the opposite end of the bench.

Ventura continued, "Detective, can you please recount the visit to Mr. Freeman's bench?"

"Thank you, Dr. Ventura."

Detective Jackman was an attractive woman, in her early forties. She had professionally styled dark, shoulder-length hair. Her fit figure was accentuated in her well-tailored gray business suit. She reached for the microphone in the middle of the table and pulled it toward her.

She cleared her throat, introduced herself, and began giving the details of her visit to the bench.

"When I got to the park and found the bench where people were waiting to talk to Mr. Freeman, I stood until a spot opened up to sit."

"How many people were there to visit him?" Ventura inquired.

"There was four total, including me, and the one he was already talking to. The people waiting were of different ethnicities and genders."

With only four people, Jonah wondered how many different races and genders there could've been?

She continued, "When it came time for me to go to the bench, he welcomed me over and had me sit down. He gave me a cursory overview of the few rules involved."

"What were those rules, Ms. Jackman?" Ventura asked.

"I could not tell him of anything that would be a crime and he could not give me legal advice or advice. He was just there to listen.

"I started telling him a story that wasn't totally fabricated so there would be a basis of truth."

"What did you tell him?" Ventura questioned.

"I told him about the trouble I was having with my fifteen-year-old daughter. That she was going through a rebellious stage and had an older boyfriend. I told him that my daughter and I used to be close, but I was very distraught because now we rarely talked. I also told him that my husband didn't seem to be engaged so I felt alone and doing the parenting all on my own."

Now, he remembered her! She had given him much more detail at the bench than she was giving now. He believed there was much more truth to her venting to him than she was alluding to at this time. The detail let him believe she was using her meeting with him to actually get some things off her chest.

"How long did you speak to Mr. Freeman?" Ventura asked.

"Probably fifteen minutes. Others were waiting."

"How did the session end?"

Jonah thought it was prejudicial to call it a 'session', but they were in a hearing, not a real trial so his attorney (who wasn't there) couldn't object.

"He asked me something like was I glad I talked to him. Then he said something about teenagers being tough and maybe I should talk to my husband as I had to him."

Ventura jumped in, "So it sounds as though you're saying he gave you some advice after all?"

Jackman thought for a second, then responded, "I can't say for sure if he did or didn't. I mean he did tell me those things, but it was more as if he was a friend telling a friend, not some formal advice."

"But he did give you advice?" Ventura badgered.

"Well, yes. I guess."

She was questioned for several more minutes including questions from the other two doctors who had been eerily quiet up until this point. When it appeared that they had gotten all they needed from the detective, Dr. Ventura finished. "Thank you for your time, Detective Jackman. You are excused."

Nancy Jackman collected her things and stood up. As she walked toward the back of the room and passed Jonah, she looked secretly at him and smiled, slightly out of the view of the officials.

A break was announced after the detective left. Jonah used the opportunity to go to the bathroom and get a drink of water. With a few minutes left, he headed toward the balcony overlooking the lobby below. The elevators were there and so was Detective Jackman. She saw him and although slightly startled, she also seemed happy to see him.

She looked around to make sure no one was watching. There wasn't. It was just the two of them. "Look, Mr. Freeman. I just want you to know that even though I was officially working undercover at the time, I do believe talking to you helped me with some of my problems. I was able to talk things over with my husband and we became more of a united front after that. Thank you."

"I'm glad it helped."

Her elevator opened, "Good luck, Mr. Freeman."

The doors closed and she was gone.

Jonah returned to the boardroom newly justified in what he was doing. Round two was about to start and it would be his.

As he settled into his chair, only Dr. Lab Coat was at the head of the table. Jonah nodded. The man looked away. Soon the other two doctors and the two clerical people returned, one man, and one woman. Jonah guessed they were students of Dr. Ventura helping her with administrative parts of the hearing. Neither of them interacted with him, as instructed.

Dr. Ventura sat at the end of the table, cleared her throat, and began to speak. "Mr. Freeman, we now want to hear from you. We will then invite you to leave after which we will continue the hearing amongst my colleagues.

Jonah nodded showing he understood.

"Mr. Freeman, you had said earlier that you have had experience with counseling. Would you mind letting us know the circumstances of your therapy and what the outcome was?"

He replied, "No, I did not say that I had therapy or any kind of counseling. I said I was familiar with it because of members of my family. I will not go into that with you as it is not my story to tell."

"Do you feel the members of your family received value from the therapy?" She asked.

"I do. It was at a time and place where they needed help. With therapy along with medication, she eventually became better."

308

Ventura probed, "Why were you not able to give her the therapy she needed?"

It was obvious where she was going with this line of questioning. Jonah responded, "I certainly tried, but I was not trained in a way to know what to do. She attended therapy at the recommendation of our family doctor. That's all I'm willing to say about her situation."

"I understand" was the first cordial thing she had said to him.

"Jonah, if you did not feel qualified and trained to help this person in your life who you knew very well, what has changed to think you are qualified to counsel these complete strangers in the park?"

It was interesting that she was calling him by his first name. Had she somehow seen him as an individual and not just the subject of her investigation?

Jonah calmly took a breath to hold his disdain. He spoke respectively, "I've told you all more than once that I do not provide therapy. I rarely give advice and when I do it's because they have asked. Even in those times, I am careful in what I say."

For the first time, Dr. Sanchez leaned forward to speak. "Dr. Ventura, if I may ask a question, please. Mr. Freeman, have you ever considered what impact your discussion with these strangers has? In other words, what do they do after they leave? How do they change or proceed with life?"

"When we are through, I almost always asked them if they are glad they talked to me. Almost unanimously, they answer in the affirmative. They seem lightened by a burden in which they had nowhere else to turn."

"So, you do not believe there is anywhere else for them to go besides you, an untrained man sitting on a park bench with the pigeons?"

"Because of your condescension, I will be addressing my answers to Dr. Ventura. I can't determine which of you asks the questions, but I can control to whom I answer."

Dr. Ventura seemed empowered by Jonah taking the conversation back to her. He proceeded to answer Dr. Jerk Face's question, "I have no way of knowing what resources these people have or who they have in their lives. I am simply responding to their need for someone to talk to at that moment in time."

Dr. Sanchez continued his line of questioning even after Jonah tried to put him in his place. "Mr. Freeman, you seem to have some contempt for the psychiatric community. Is that because of a negative experience you've had or because you may have not grown up in an atmosphere where education was valued, and you were not taught the importance of seeking out experts?"

Jonah was seething inside, but he knew he could do better for himself by simply taking him head-on. "Mr. Sanchez, first of all, I find a hint of racism in your statement. Just because I'm black, you assume these things."

This put Sanchez back on his heels a little. He—a Hispanic man — being accused of making a statement based on race, did not sit well with him.

"As a matter of fact, I was raised in a home where education was considered paramount. I would put my upbringing against yours, without even knowing yours. My mother and father were both professors at the University of Colorado. My two brothers both have received post-graduate degrees. In my family alone there are four bachelor's degrees, four master's degrees, and two doctorates. Dr. Ventura, would your colleague like to give me his family's background as it pertains to education?"

After a pause for him not to answer, he continued, "I didn't think so."

That was the last comment heard from Dr. Sanchez.

"But to answer his question about having contempt, I have no negative feelings at all about your profession. There is definitely a need. Mental illness seems to be almost an epidemic in our country. It's going to take more than just talking things out or watching a funny movie to heal. People with mental illness need to be able to work through their issues with professionals and even be prescribed medication if they need it. On more than one occasion, I have suggested to friends of mine that they should seek help. Long before mental health was routinely covered on insurance policies, I was instrumental in getting our company to include it in the company's coverage. There is a huge need for caring professionals in your arena. There are definitely diagnosable conditions that need the help of professionals like yourself.

"Having said that, I also don't believe that every issue needs to be resolved with a visit to a psychiatrist or therapist. In my short time listening in the park, I find that most of these people aren't seeking out advice. They are simply wanting someone to talk to, someone to tell. In most cases, they have not been able to tell anyone in their circle, either because of the sensitivity of the subject or their embarrassment.

"The number one thing people talk to me about is loneliness. That is not something your profession can help them with. You cannot be their friend. As a matter of fact, you steer from being their friend because it crosses a doctor/patient line. Going to you does not fulfill that need. Granted, I don't generally become their friend either, but there have been cases where they have become a friend.

"What I do on the bench beside the pigeons is not meant to fix people's problems. I am there to hear what they need to say. Many times, there is very little conversation after they speak. They just thank me and walk away in a little happier place.

"Not everyone needs to be fixed—some just need to be heard. In those cases, mine are the ears they seek."

The room was quiet. Jonah was not sure if his words were so strong that the doctors were fuming with the chastisement or if they were actually contemplating what he said. Whether he helped or hurt his case, he really couldn't say and frankly, didn't care. Maybe legally Jonah needed their approval, but personally he did not.

The three doctors huddled again mumbling incoherently.

Jonah caught the glance of the male student who quickly looked away. The female student peeked at him with a gentle smile.

They turned back to Jonah and Dr. Ventura spoke, "Mr. Freeman, that concludes the portion of our hearing where we are receiving testimony. Do you have anything else you want us to take into consideration?"

He did not. He thanked them for allowing him to attend and walked stoically out of the boardroom. It was now out of his hands. There was nothing else he could do.

One of Jonah's life values is to always be in control and accept responsibility for his situation in life. He knew he was generally happier when he accepted accountability for those things that happen to him in his life—good or bad—and realize they are often just consequences of choices he has made. He always thought when things that happen to him are totally out of his control, he can still choose how he will react to them, thus still in control.

Jonah felt as though he had represented himself well and had done all he could to help determine the outcome.

Chapter 22

Revealing His Verdict

The time had come for Jonah to meet with his friends and let them know of his situation. He had asked Patrick, Marvin, and Pam to meet him the next morning at the north end of the park, away from the Listening Bench.

Normally this time of year, one can always count on a cool morning but ample sunshine. On this morning, the sky was overcast and there was a sense of impending rain. Once everyone had arrived, they sat at a cold cement picnic table in the center of the park away from the morning runners, walkers, and bikers. Jonah had brought coffee for everyone and set it in the center of the table. Well, coffee for three and hot chocolate for Pam who he knew didn't drink coffee.

The small talk was subtle. They assumed he was meeting with them to tell them about the results of the hearing and by his somber nature, it couldn't be good.

Jonah began, "Thank you for making the arrangements to be here this morning. I wanted to meet at this place in the park to give us the most privacy."

They were waiting for the news. The news they heard was nothing they expected.

"First of all, I know you all want to know about the hearing. Well, there is nothing to tell really. I just answered their questions and had a chance to tell them my side of the story. I got a call from the D.A.'s office this morning saying that there should be a decision within a month."

While his coffee was still cooling, he took the lid off of his bottled water and took a sip simply to moisten his dry mouth.

"So, you're probably wondering why I wanted to meet with you if not for news on the hearing.

"I need you all to know something that will affect how we proceed with the bench from here on out.

"You have all become very dear friends. I have other great friends from my life before the bench, but I feel I've gotten to share this experience with the three of you in a completely different way."

It was time to give them his life's verdict.

"The truth is, I'm dying."

This announcement was met with a gasp from Patrick, an 'oh no' from Pam, and simply a direct gaze from Marvin's glistening eyes.

"What do you mean?" Marvin asked somberly.

"Not long after I started doing the listening thing, I went to my family doctor because of some pain I was having below my ribs. After a series of tests, an oncologist revealed I have stage four liver cancer. I guess liver cancer is hard to detect and is one of the fastest progressing cancers. I reviewed it with a team of doctors as to what my options were."

Jonah was unsure how much of his explanation Pam heard as she was taking the news hard.

"They said it was terminal and would soon take my life. There were indeed some treatments they could perform, but at the end of the day, the treatments would only prolong the inevitable and not give me a very good quality of life in the meantime.

"You've probably noticed I've been missing more and more days here. Thank you, Marvin and Pam, for filling in. The pain and nausea are increasing in a way that I just can't go on.

"The day Patrick told me about the investigation was the same day that the doctor told me the end was near. I would start quickly deteriorating and would soon need hospice. It was very sobering news as you can imagine. I drove up into the canyons and took one last hike. It was hard, but it was fitting.

"My mom is coming out to be with me for the final days."

The group was in shock. Patrick was the first to come to him. Jonah stood up and they hugged. He cried hard but controlled. He told Jonah he loved him. Jonah believed it. Next, Pam rushed over and held him harder than she probably should've hugged a man with the pain of cancer. She was not handling it well, so he let her stay that way as long as needed.

Finally, Marvin walked over to Jonah, hugged him gently, and simply thanked him for helping him find purpose in his life. He thanked his friend for introducing him to Veronica and said he felt they were developing a great companionship.

After several minutes passed and the tears subsided, Jonah spoke again.

"I also wanted to meet with you about some unfinished business. I'm not worried about the investigation. I will probably be gone before it is decided, but I do want to talk to you three about where this all goes from here. I think what we've got going on here is very important and I don't want to see it end.

"Patrick, after I'm gone, I would request you write an article about how the Listening Bench will proceed without me heading it up. I don't think it's fair to put the weight on either Pam or Marvin. Pam has a job and is soon to be married. Marvin is exploring the early stages of a new relationship and needs to concentrate on some level to that.

"So here is my plan. See what you think and I'm open to feedback. "Not realizing they were leaning in, his friends were intrigued and listening to every word. "Pam and Marvin, if you could keep doing what you are doing until I...pass and Patrick writes the article, I would appreciate that. Even if you have to cut back to once or twice a week, we shouldn't lose our momentum.

"In the long run, would you agree, that it isn't necessarily *us* the people need? They just need a listener. Someone to care enough to hear them out. A friend in confidence even if just for a few minutes."

Pam and Marvin both agreed.

"So, what I'm thinking is to make anyone who could be a listener participate."

All three looked at Jonah with questioning anticipation for him to explain further.

"My thought is this. Patrick will reveal the new procedure in his article. Pam and Marvin devise a way to communicate it after my death. Maybe flyers are handed or posted at the pavilions.

"Again, to the plan. Anyone who wants to be a listener will get a nametag like one would get at a convention, that simply has an ear on it. It signifies that they are willing to listen to anyone that needs to talk. I want the nametags to be purple, something that stands out. The listeners won't be tied to a bench or a time of day. They wear it around on their chest while they are at the park as their way of announcing their availability."

"Let that sink in for a minute while I get a drink."

After a minute or so, Marvin spoke, "That is a wonderful plan. No one will get in trouble with the law since these people are just talking one on one with people and not soliciting for any one listener. They can't come after us all."

Pam joined in. "I really support the idea too, but one thing is worrying me. How do we qualify these people to be listeners?"

Jonah replied, "I don't think we do. How do you qualify people to be a friend? We don't. One thing that might help, is when you hand out the purple nametag with the ear, you also hand them a sheet of ideas on how to be an effective listener. Things that we have all learned."

"These are the details you can work out over the next four to six weeks."

His calling out the time frame brought the discussion back to him.

Patrick was the first to ask, "How are you doing with all of this, Jonah?"

He didn't have to think long because he dealt with these feelings every day. "Well, I'll give you the negatives first. I'm sure it's the same with all people who are facing death. Part of me is scared, not necessarily about dying but what my life will be leading up to death. I'm disappointed that both Michelle and I won't make it out of our fifties. We talked so much about what we were going to do in retirement, but apparently, it isn't meant to be.

"These last several months have been great for me, a renaissance of sorts. All my life, I looked for purpose in my career, but in the last few months, I feel I've actually made a difference. I wish I could've seen it continue."

Jonah hugged each of them again and let them know he would be in touch. He worked out some more details with Patrick about his end of life and the article he would write.

Jonah walked to the other end of the park and sat on his bench overlooking the lake. So much had happened on this spot during the past several months. So many confessions, secrets, and thoughts were shared.

As he was beginning to get up, an old man came to him and asked, "Are you the man people talk to? I need to get some burdens off my chest."

"Of course. Please sit down." Jonah said as he talked to his last Fide.

Randy Judd

Epilogue

Patrick had previously written the article so he was able to publish it on the day I passed. He titled the piece, *The Art of the Listening Bench*. I liked that. He compared what we had done to a great artist who created a tapestry of love and acceptance for those who needed to be heard. That was very nice of him. I was humbled to have that much attention.

I had reviewed my will with Patrick. I left all of my estate to *Angelforward*. My initial endowment would put me well ahead of Lawyer Boley for years to come. Patrick wanted to change the name to *The Jonah Freeman Memorial Fund*. I wouldn't let him. We settled on *The Listening Bench Fund*.

Patrick and Tim were happy to take Wilhelm into their home. My dog was getting old and needed a place to convalesce. I knew they would treat him well.

My funeral was the Tuesday after my death. Not a lot happened the last month. I was medicated most of the time, but after death, I felt SO free!

I thought I would stay around a little bit longer to honor those who took time out of their day to attend my funeral. The ones who spoke said some nice things. I know I wasn't as good as they said, but I also know everyone is several degrees better in a eulogy. I hated seeing people cry, but I know that is part of death and separation. If they only knew how good I felt now, they might not be so inclined to mourn. We tend to mourn at someone's death not necessarily for the person who died, but for those left behind and their longing. We won't be seeing each other in the near future at all. My body was laid next to my wonderful Michelle. I was happy to see the fresh flowers from my grave spill over to hers. She deserved them more.

The Listening Bench

One of the last things I did was go by Liberty Park. I was taken back and humbled by what I saw. In the park, there are perhaps seventy-five benches, all near walking paths and most in the shade. To my pleasant surprise, more than half of them had two people on them, one having a purple nametag with an ear on it. Each listener had taken it upon themselves to continue what I had started so many months ago. It would take the new listeners a while to get the hang of it, but not too long. Being an effective listener is not really that hard. The listener just needs to pay attention. They just need to care about the person in front of them and be in the moment. They shouldn't think about the next thing they're going to say, just pay attention to what the other person is saying. The listener needs to not only show compassion and interest, but most importantly, they should FEEL compassion. They need to realize the person came to them for one purpose, to get something off their mind. In the end, all they need to do to be an effective listener....is LISTEN.

It's funny how life turns out. I worked most of my life in a job that had great importance to the company, and except for helping provide a good living for Michelle and me, did not provide much fulfillment to my inner soul. It's as I've said before, sometimes you don't find your calling, but the calling finds you. Then, in the last nine months of my life, even without my wonderful wife beside me, I found self-actualization. I felt I had made a difference in the world, at least in my small part of it.

I'm reminded of the story of the little boy walking along the beach who was picking up starfish which had been abandoned by the tide and then throwing them back in the water.

"You can't make a difference, son," a man who was walking by said, "there are too many. You'll never save them all."

The boy looked at the many starfish spread out before him and picked up another one.

"I can't make a difference to them all," the boy said throwing the one he had into the sea, "but I made a difference to that one."

I feel I have made an impact. I could not help them all, but hopefully, I made a difference to some.

My time had come. It was time to move on to my next chapter. Just as I finished rejoicing at the scene in the park, I felt her familiar hand gently resting on my shoulder. I turned to experience whatever lay ahead for us.

The End

Thank you for reading my novel. I'm happy to have shared it with you. I would appreciate your thoughts in a review on Amazon and Goodreads. An honest review will help other readers in their decisions and will help me in developing future projects.

I invite you to read my first novel:

<u>The Art of Straightening Nails</u>

Also available on Amazon

Thank you,

Randy